T0297208

Millennium

and other short stories

Matthew Theisen

iUniverse, Inc.
New York Bloomington

Millennium
and other short stories

Copyright © 2009 Matthew Theisen

All rights reserved. No part of this book may be used or reproduced by any means, graphic, electronic, or mechanical, including photocopying, recording, taping or by any information storage retrieval system without the written permission of the publisher except in the case of brief quotations embodied in critical articles and reviews.

This is a work of fiction. All of the characters, names, incidents, organizations, and dialogue in this novel are either the products of the author's imagination or are used fictitiously.

iUniverse books may be ordered through booksellers or by contacting:

iUniverse
1663 Liberty Drive
Bloomington, IN 47403
www.iuniverse.com
1-800-Authors (1-800-288-4677)

Because of the dynamic nature of the Internet, any Web addresses or links contained in this book may have changed since publication and may no longer be valid. The views expressed in this work are solely those of the author and do not necessarily reflect the views of the publisher, and the publisher hereby disclaims any responsibility for them.

ISBN: 978-1-4401-7087-4 (pbk)
ISBN: 978-1-4401-7088-1 (ebook)

Printed in the United States of America

iUniverse rev. date: 9/3/09

I.

Love is Perjured Everywhere

Bernadette turned from the television screen and the fellow beside her who was trying to engage her in conversation. "Uh-oh," she said, and walked over to the table where a young woman was being posed to the raucous singing of the men.

"Do you like those scum-stained teeth?"

"Yes, we like those scum-stained teeth!"

Irving was standing beside the young woman, pointing to various parts of her anatomy. The girl's friend, left out of the circle of chanting males, was crying quietly, not wishing to attract the men by protesting the treatment of her gal-pal.

Happens every year, Bernadette thought, and they seem to be getting younger. She pushed through the men, ignoring the pat on her rump, and carefully pulled the girl off the table, steered her through the ring of disappointed males- who voiced their disapproval loudly- and joined the cowering brunette in a skirt- of all things!- who grabbed her friend and let Bernadette lead them sobbing to the front door.

"Animals!" the blonde shouted, wiping her nose on her sleeve. "How could they do that?"

"Now you know what a rugby party is like," Bernadette said. "It's part of your college experience."

"They said there'd be a lot of other women," the brunette said, her savage face looming like a fury's, reflecting the multi-colored bar lights.

"And you believed them?" Bernadette asked.

They wept in tandem and lurched down the stone steps to the sidewalk. "You're not going back in there, are you?" the blonde asked.

"One of those animals is my boyfriend."

"Oh, lucky you!" the brunette cried out as the blonde sobbed a laugh.

Bernadette returned to her barstool, thinking the girls at least had enough sense to not show up alone, as one young lady had a few years previous; Bernadette had mercilessly let her suffer through several songs before rescuing her.

Their prey gone, the men started another song, which didn't require a sacrificial victim:
"Bang bang Lulu, Lulu bangs all day

who we gonna bang on when Lulu goes away?"

"Where'd the Mexican guy go?" Bernadette asked Celeste.

"He's Indian. He took off while you were saving the girl."

"How do you know he's Indian?"

"I asked him earlier. What were you two talking about?"

Bernadette shook her head. "I'm not sure. He was getting kind of drunk and asked which I preferred: Ovid or Darwin."

"Huh?"

"It was something about how species get started." Bernadette inclined her head, "I'll give him credit: he's a smart guy. I didn't think I'd ever meet someone who read Ovid in this place."

"Have you read Ovid?"

"No, but I know who he is. He wrote about people becoming plants and animals."

Ten minutes later, Irving sidled up to Bernadette and said to Celeste, "More beer for the troops."

"Hold on, Celeste; I need to talk with him a second."

"Talk while she's filling the pitchers. You know I can't read your sign language."

"I was waving you over here for the past twenty minutes to tell you those girls might have gotten back to their dorm and decided they've been assaulted. While we're at it, besides them being underage and angry enough to call the cops, how many guys on the team are underage?"

Irving sank next to her and said quietly, "No more beer, Celeste." He wiped his face slowly, the sweat dripping from his fingers. Then he became a dervish, whirling quickly around the bar, turning off lights and shoving his team out the door. The groans and catcalls only spurred him to rage, "This is my place and I'm not going to lose my liquor license because some 18-year-old can't handle it! Now get out! Holy Christ! Who left Trevor in the goddamn bathroom alone with his head in the toilet bowl? You guys said you'd take care of him and he's drowning like a sewer rat!"

Minutes later, the team heading for a party in someone's apartment amidst mutterings of Irving being a grouchy old fart, Dennis emerged from the backroom where he had been playing pool alone.

"Run 'em all out, didja?"

"Yeah. Fer Chrissake, why didn't you help?"

"I was working on my game. I think I might give up rugby for something a little more sedate."

"Sedate, huh?"

Dennis sat next to him and they both watched Celeste clean up the plastic cups scattered about the tavern. Eventually, Irving turned to Bernadette and said, "What is this? The silent treatment?"

"I'm watching this."

"No you're not; you're just staring at it."

"Oh, I forgot. You can read minds now."

"Awright then, what is it?"

"It's a play."

"Well I can see that. What is it though?"

"Shakespeare."

"Oh. Ohhhh. *Shakespeare.* I didn't know there's a play called *Shakespeare.*"

Bernadette looked at Irving, shook her head and said, "Don't be such an ass."

"Well you don't even know the title. Come on, let's switch it to the sports' station."

Abruptly, the screen fizzed with static and Bernadette looked for the remote control, yelling, "Hey, I'm serious! I was watching that!"

"I didn't change channels."

"Well, who did?"

Dennis nodded at the screen, "It's him. Captain Pirate."

Irving and Bernadette released Ohs of realization.

Captain Pirate was the popular regional name of a video genius who could engage all the earth's airwaves for singular moments when he appeared onscreen, in various guises, spouting all kinds of insane rubbish. He first showed up as a hunter garbed in green and brown leaves and branches, complete with bow and quiver; his hair was shock red and he howled in furious Sanskrit, which was interpreted into the appropriate subtitles in every area's dialect,

"Heed my warning, you little bilious monsters! I will hunt you down and feed your ravenous corpses to the great gluttonous womb of Kali!"

Needless to say, the world was stunned. Imitators immediately sprang up and were quickly nabbed by the authorities. Rumors spread with each appearance. The more imaginative- or gullible- thought him to be a space alien whose science transcended that of earth's. The conspiracy buffs believed he was a former government technician who got tired of routine lab work and expanded, like a franchise, to make the entire globe his experiment.

Irving and Bernadette had been gloriously high when Captain Pirate showed up as a snarling Asian in full body armor, shouting Mongolian oaths that he would herd all of humanity into this stables as if they were ponies. The next day, Irving and Bernadette swore off marijuana until Captain Pirate could be brought to justice.

However, despite the government's reassurances, there he was: a corpulent man in a purple overcoat that was lined with ribbons and medals, shouting in German, "I will track you like the beasts on my estate, but even the most worthy of you do not warrant a position of honor as a trophy in my hunting lodge. You are mere fodder for my energy."

"Jesus, a Nazi?" Dennis said.

The regular programming returned a few moments later and Irving said, "I think I liked him best as the Indian in the cowboy outfit. What language was he speaking? Huh? Hey, Bern, I asked what-"

"I heard you. They think it was some dialect of Mayan or Aztec."

"Yeah. He was like at the Alamo or something."

Dennis nodded, "That one was good, but I preferred the hairy guy in the bearskin… Nimrod was what the press called him."

"What a great name," Irving said. "Well, what should we do?"

"We could go to my parents' cabin," Dennis suggested.

"Good idea. Let's swing by and get our rifles."

"Okay. But this time we'll have to chop some wood. My parents keep complaining about it."

"Chop wood," Bernadette snorted. "You mean play around with a chainsaw."

"What sissies!" Irving exclaimed, looking at the TV. He paused in beery reflection. "Why do they always get homos to play straight leads?"

"Oh, listen to Mr. I Love Being At The Bottom Of A Scrum."

"Aw, don't start that psychological crap on me," Irving sighed, leaning an elbow on the bar and rubbing his face with a paw. "I mean, what's next with all the Shakespeare revisions? A queer *Romeo and Juliet*?"

"How would you know?" Bernadette asked. "You can't even sit through a normal version."

"Even the normal versions are full of shit," Irving sneered. "You were so keen on seeing *Hamlet* and they had blacks in it. Now how many blacks were in- where was it?"

"Denmark," Celeste answered from where she was wiping off a table.

"Right. And it was set in like 1400. Why not do a revision of *Roots* starring whites as slaves?"

"They could be Irish and England would be the oppressor," Dennis said.

"Yeah," Irving said. "Now we're swinging. You know, all the European countries bragging about getting rid of slavery before the U.S. did is nonsense. They just didn't want a bunch of nig-nogs in their dinky little countries so made it illegal in their own nations and went out to colonize the wogs and chinks in their own lands."

"Do you have to ruin everything I like?" Bernadette asked.

"I'm just saying it's like having a chick play Peter Pan."

"Now we're more at your cultural level," she replied. "Besides, men used to play the women in Shakespeare's time."

"Okay then," Irving said, "you've exactly proven my point. Shakespeare sucks because he wrote the women's roles knowing a man would be playing the part. It started the whole trend of fags on parade. Now they're everywhere, especially in theater."

Bernadette said, "Mr. Homophobe strikes again. And by the way, if it wasn't for men making all those laws barring women from playing parts, then maybe things would be more to your liking."

"Queen Elizabeth was a woman," Dennis said mildly. "Unless she was in drag too."

"But she was stuck in a patriarchal society," Celeste said.

"Bullshit," Irving said. "She didn't want to- what's the word?- empower women because she didn't want the competition." He leaned back from the bar and asked, "Who's driving? I know I'm not."

"I will," Celeste said.

Dennis volunteered, "I can drive."

"Oh no. Not another roller-coaster ride," Celeste said. "We're lucky you didn't pile us in a tree last time."

"A show of hands," Irving announced. "All in favor of Celeste? Ah, looks like you lose, buddy. I'll go unlock the backdoor so we can make our escape. Celeste, you can finish cleaning up tomorrow."

"Gee, thanks."

Irving stood and went towards the back of the tavern. "What's with all the sarcasm tonight? Must be something in the water."

"Well try some," Bernadette called. "All you've had the past two days is beer." After Irving made his exit, and Celeste went into the small kitchen to clean herself, Bernadette turned to Dennis and asked, "Who told the guys my nickname is- was- Big Boobs Bernadette?"

Dennis looked up from his beer and said, "Oh, you heard that, huh?"

"Yes, I heard that, huh," she mimicked. "You know, I didn't mind it much when I was younger, but I'm 24 now and I'm not going to go through life with guys chanting 'BBB' every time I walk in a room."

"Well I don't know who told them. I think it just kind of filtered down from the older guys."

"You *are* the older guys."

Dennis shifted uneasily, "I meant like the upper classmen."

"You've been hanging out with Irving for years and you still haven't learned how to lie like him."

"I honestly don't know who started it." They sat in silence for a moment, then Dennis said, "I suppose that's another reason for the operation."

"I suppose that's right," Bernadette said, straightening her back with a wince.

"Irving will be crushed."

"He'll get over it. And there's always his girly books."

"Hey," Irving returned, "what are you talking about?"

"How my mom stopped by after church last Sunday and there were stacks of pornography in our living room."

"He doesn't need to know that. Besides, I was moving them into the garage."

"So why are they still there?"

"I haven't picked up the boxes and bubble-wrap yet. I don't want them to get mildew."

"The one thing in the house he cares about."

"Bernadette…" Irving shook his head and became silent.

Celeste came from the kitchen, untying her apron, "All right. Let's go."

*** *** ***

The bonfire in the outside pit was small but warm. They had argued on previous occasions on the subject of music and came to the conclusion that the cabin would be a place free of such acrimony as to whose turn it was to choose the tunes; which suited Irving, for he could always rely on claiming the tavern as his castle and the reigning muses to be those whom he so dubbed.

Celeste and Bernadette shared gossip about Saint Johns College, where the former was taking classes in children's education. Dennis interrupted them to say, "What we have to ask ourselves is our children being educated?"

Bernadette laughed, "Not by you, Mr. Grammarian."

Dennis shook his head slowly, "I was only asking the same thing our figurehead of education asked when he ran for president."

"Oh, that's right," Celeste said. "Geez, what a moron."

"Hey," Irving said. "I voted for him."

"We know, Irv," Bernadette soothed; "and you have our condolences."

"Education is overrated," Irving said. "It's all about popular cults nowadays. I really don't think Shakespeare sucks, I just see him being used to herd the masses into smug shrines of self-worship to further their own agendas."

"Self-worship is what you specialize in," Bernadette said, taking Irving's hand in hers.

"What kind of agenda is Shakespeare used to perpetuate?" Celeste asked.

"You dragged me to that movie of some actor playing Shakespeare having sex while spouting poetry, remember?"

"Yeah. So?"

"Well," Irving said, "part of the point was bad-daddyism and how oppressed women were. It completely skipped over Catholicism being an outlawed religion."

Bernadette ran a hand over her face, "Irving, it was a movie. Do you really think people would understand the politics of England developing its own religion and banning Catholics?"

"The real problem is Americans have too much leisure time," Irving expounded: "We spend energy worrying about how future generations will view us as parent figures, like King Henry VIII But all we're really doing is just making one-dimensional screen mommies and daddies who don't care about anything except enhancing their self-image."

"Where'd you get that from?" Bernadette asked.

Irving leaned forward to poke a stick at the fire, then sat back in his lawn-chair. "The guy who runs the comic book shop down the street came in for a beer- well, more like ten or fifteen- the other day before we got busy. He's a smart guy, even if he's a raging alcoholic. Anyway, as you might guess from his job, he's big into hero worship."

"Knowledge from comic book geeks," Bernadette said. "My, you are diverse."

"Actually, I thought of most of it myself. He was just the uh...catalyst. See, men used to have true war heroes as their icons, but thirty years of peace- with intermittent media wars- has changed the fabric of men into celebrity worshippers. It's what we get educated to support: popular cults."

"What about the wars in Iraq and Afghanistan?"

"Right," Dennis laughed. "How many generals do you see leading the charge? They're all on TV talking about how great they're doing."

"Hey, look," Celeste called. "The Aurora Borealis. You can just see it over the treetops. It's like a red curtain forms and then pulls open."

"The gods must be watching us on stage," Dennis said.

Irving asked, "You remember what that guy from Marquette said about Galileo?"

"Oh yeah. The physicist."

"A physicist rugby player?" Bernadette said.

"He was their kicker," Dennis replied. "We got really high after the game and he went on and on about reincarnation. Said Galileo was reborn as Isaac Newton; after having learned his lesson not to go against a religion's beliefs, he got tenure at...Cambridge, I think, where he didn't have to teach classes."

Irving laughed, "Yeah, all the educating was done by people who didn't understand Newton's theories. In other words, the morons."

"Thanks a lot," Celeste said.

"Aw, I didn't mean it like that."

"Yes you did, so don't bother apologizing."

"Irving thinks he was Rommel in a previous life," Dennis said.

"Who?" Bernadette asked.

"A German field commander," Dennis said. "The Desert Fox."

"A Nazi?" Bernadette exclaimed. "You think you were a Nazi?"

"He wasn't a Nazi," Irving replied. "He never joined the party. In fact, he was part of the conspiracy to kill Hitler."

"Must have been watching the History Channel."

"No," Irving said. "You're wrong again."

"Well then where'd you learn about whatshisname?"

"You don't know everything I do. I happen to have a library card."

"I've seen him reading at work," Celeste told her.

"Well. Why don't you bring them home?"

"Because I'd never get them read."

Dennis said, "After that life, Irving was Martin Luther King Junior."

Irving laughed. "I forgot I told you that."

"That Marquette guy had everybody going on about past lives."

"Wait a minute," Bernadette said: "Mr. Nigger This And Nigger That thinks he was black?"

Irving shook his head, "They're just words. And blacks use them all the time so I'm just being one of them."

"You nigger," Dennis laughed.

"That's me," Irving agreed. "But you're not allowed to say it because you're not one of us."

"According to Irving," Dennis said, "he lost respect for authority, racism, and bad leadership during World War II, so he got reincarnated as a general of a different kind of combat."

"That's right," Irving said. "And now that the world is on the brink of the apocalypse, I'm retiring from every battle except what I choose. The fun ones."

Celeste said, "Well, if you like George Bush Junior so much, why not join the military and fight for his crusades?"

"Who said I like him? Voting for someone doesn't mean you like them. I just couldn't stand four years of Al Gore talking to me- and everyone else- like we're all three-year-old retards. This way I feel smarter than the president."

The others laughed and Dennis passed around some beer.

"I'm fading fast," Irving said.

"Yeah," Bernadette agreed. "Let's go get some sleep."

*** *** ***

The next morning the four had breakfast in the cabin. Irving and Celeste had already showered and dressed; Dennis was in a robe and Bernadette was wearing a sweat suit.

Bernadette, a lover of metaphysics, said, "I had a strange dream last night. We were supposed to be in school but were playing hooky."

"Oh yeah?" Dennis asked. "Where'd we go?"

"To a carnival. And there was a puppet show going on that was about us."

Dennis: "Did we like become the puppets?"

"It sure seemed as if something was controlling us."

Irving swallowed some eggs and toast, then said, "Maybe it's a sign you shouldn't go back to school."

"Or a sign that I should quit hanging around you riff-raff."

Celeste laughed, "We're a bad influence on you."

Irving grumbled wordlessly and Bernadette said, "While you guys go hunting, I'm going to have Celeste help me choose some classes." She turned to her friend, "I brought the St. John's catalogue for next semester."

"She's been carrying it with her for a month," Irving said. "She woke up puking the other day and I asked if she had morning sickness."

"That's Mr. Sympathy for you."

"We'll do it tonight, Bernadette," Celeste said. "I'm going hunting with the guys."

"You are?"

"Yeah. I'm going to be Irving's gun-bearer. Right, Bwana?"

"That's right," Irving said. "Did you bring your license?"

"It's in my wallet," Dennis said.

"Are you sure?"

"Yeah. I don't want to get caught poaching again. Here it…no, that's not it. Where is it? I'm gonna go check the car." A few minutes later, Dennis returned. "I don't know where the hell it is. I could've sworn I had it in my wallet."

"It's probably at home," Celeste said.

"I guess it's just you and me then," said Irving.

"Right," Celeste agreed. "Let's go."

The two left the cabin, Celeste carrying Irving's rifle.

"What do you suppose those two are up to?" Dennis asked.

"Don't be an ass," Bernadette replied.

"I'm going to check the car and see if they took the blanket."

"Why bother?"

"Because I know I had my hunting license in my wallet and tonight I'll probably find it in my dresser under some socks."

"Well, I'm going to work on my class schedule. You go ahead and play detective."

"Aren't you even a little bothered?"

"Yes, Dennis, I'm very bothered. But I'm not married and they don't seem to mind what we do so I'm not going to mind- at least not out loud- what they do."

"You think they know?"

“Let’s not talk about it,” Bernadette said. “It makes me feel like I’m in a sordid soap opera.”

“I thought you liked them; arranged your work schedule around your favorites.”

She shrugged, “I used to, but I’ve given up on them.”

Dennis asked, “When did this happen?”

“Oh, it’s been a while now. I didn’t quit cold turkey; I just sort of weaned myself from them.”

“Now you’re into Shakespeare, huh?” Bernadette shrugged again and Dennis said, “Well, I’m not as sophisticated as you; I’m going to look in the car.”

Dennis returned with a blanket and a bottle of wine.

“Excellent,” Bernadette said. “Put it in the freezer to get it cold. Now be quiet. I have to choose some classes.”

“I thought you were going to have Celeste help you.”

“You might not be able to tell, but right now she’s not one of my favorite people.”

“Is she still going with you when you have the operation?”

“I don’t know. And right now, I don’t care. Pretty soon she’ll graduate and move to someplace like Chicago or New York and chances are I’ll never see her again. Unless you manage to marry her, in which case I’ll only see her about once a year. Either way is fine by me. I’m getting tired of hearing how small Stillwater is; as if I don’t already know.”

“But you are going through with the operation?”

“Probably. If Celeste won’t drive me to Iowa City, then my mom will.”

“Celeste will do it.”

“I don’t need to be patronized by her. Now leave me alone- but first get me a glass of wine- so I can finish this.”

“What am I supposed to do with myself? My parents even took the radio home because we forgot to lock up the last time we were here.”

“Read a book; go for a hike; swim in the river,” Bernadette said. “In other words, go out and play.”

“We don’t have any books, we’re going for a hike later, and the river’s too cold to swim in.”

“Jesus God! but you’re worse than Irving. I hate to imagine how bad it’ll be when I’m actually in school trying to study. Do you do this to Celeste?”

*** *** ***

Irving delighted in watching Celeste's tiny body tremble with joy. She was truly a marvel; each time was a unique experience.

Later, as they slowly got dressed, Celeste said, "You know, I've been thinking. You couldn't have been both Rommel and Martin Luther King Junior. I mean, the dates are all wrong."

"Celeste," Irving said, unrolling a wadded-up sock, "it was a joke. I was really high and we were talking nonsense."

"Oh. Well, Bernadette took it seriously."

"So did you if you bothered taking the time to figure out the dates of birth and death."

"You should go into the military, Irv."

"I'm too old to follow orders like the 18-year-olds. It's hard enough to keep up with them on the rugby field."

"Maybe you could be an officer."

"I'm not going to college for four years just to be an officer and fight against former allies we probably armed. Besides, college is Bernadette's thing. I'm going to have to find other things to do before I blow out a knee playing rugby and am crippled the rest of my life. I'll probably start collecting something. I mean, other than girly mags or comic books."

"Like what?" Celeste asked.

"I don't know. Maybe music or movies or sports' trivia. Or all three. Probably war books."

"Well, that's something."

"Don't waste pity on me; there's people a lot worse off."

"No," Celeste said, "I was just thinking that you read *The End of the Affair* and that was a war book."

"I meant non-fiction."

"Oh. But you did read it though."

Irving slowly shook his head, "No. No, I didn't. I was going to but to tell the truth I didn't really like the movie."

"I thought you did."

"Well, everyone else did, so I just went along."

"What didn't you like?"

"Oh, I don't know; it's been a while since we saw it."

"I can understand not liking it. I just wonder what it is you didn't like."

Irving scratched his head, "Okay. Wasn't that the movie with the dread unnamed Hollywood disease?"

"Oh. Yeah. In the book it was pneumonia."

"Right. You should've had me read the book before I saw the flick."

"I saw the movie first too." Celeste smiled brightly, "I hate it when you're right about things like that."

"It doesn't happen often."

Dennis's face was buried in a small puddle of wine on Bernadette's left breast. She briefly wondered why men always went to the left; maybe they were naturally drawn to the beat of her heart.

"Dennis, you want to go with Irving and me to see *Romeo and Juliet* at the Riverside Theater next summer?"

Dennis looked up, "Celeste will be gone. I don't want to be a third-wheel."

"You can bring someone else."

He returned his face to her breast, suckled a few moments, then asked, "What kind of version is it?"

"Well, it's *Romeo and Juliet.*"

"Yeah, but it's in Iowa City: that means it'll probably be about queers."

She pushed his head away. "You're worse than Irving. He only says stuff like that when he's drinking."

"What do you think I've been doing?"

"Acting out perverted fantasies."

"This is perversion? My, you've led a sheltered life."

"Oh, right, Mr. I've Been Around The World."

"Well, if it's a version I can stand I'll go."

Bernadette stroked his hair, "It's set in Israel is all I know."

"Oh, don't tell me," he snorted: "the great Athens of the Midwest."

"What's wrong with that? I think it's a good idea."

"Bernadette, two families fighting is quite a bit different from two religious nations at war. How could a Jew and a Muslim marrying possibly bring peace to the region?"

"Well, that's not the point."

"It should be," Dennis said. "Two Catholics getting married could stop the families' vendetta; it's plausible. Who are a Muslim and Jew gonna have act as a priest? A Buddhist? In Biblical eras, a king would make it his duty to marry a tribal princess to have a cease-fire; that's gone out of style."

"Do you have to be so literal?"

"Mmmmm...Just good old common sense. You know, that logic class I took really changed the way I look at things."

"Why don't you go back to school?"

"I might," Dennis said. "I think I'd be really good at getting inside of people's heads and messing with them. I wonder what classes cover subliminal messages. Probably advertising."

"That's what you want to do?"

"Yeah. I'd probably have to go to grad school, but I think I can handle it."

"Messing with people's minds? Yeah, you'd be good at that."

"Say, are you going to have scars?"

"The doctor said they'll be small."

"Oh," Dennis sighed.

"Why? You won't want to be with me any more?"

"No. It just seems a shame."

"Poor baby."

Dennis laughed, "Are you going to wait until after Dionysian Week at Saint Johns?"

"When is it?"

"About a month. Irving said you always double the customers then…guys, anyway."

Bernadette laughed, "You're like children going to an amusement park."

"Well, you're a local fixture, Bernadette. They could build a shrine to you and charge the pilgrims for your blessings."

"I'm sure the Catholics would love that."

"They'd be your best customers."

"Did I tell you about the old man who used to teach at Saint Johns?"

"No, I don't think so."

"Well," Bernadette said, "he comes in the tavern once in a while to sit next to me. He said I should model for the art classes. Nude, of course."

"What did he teach?"

"I'm not sure. Philosophy, I think. He just retired a few years ago."

"Oh god." Dennis laughed into her breasts making a trumpet sound. "Mr. Herd. He was my logic professor. He was always telling the girls to wear skirts; even when it was 20 below."

"He said he went through a real bitter divorce. Just like everyone else in Stillwater."

"The local curse," Dennis agreed. "The Pope could excommunicate the entire town."

"He gives the funniest reasons for coming in. 'Oh, I can't see the puck on my black and white TV,' and there isn't even a hockey game on."

Dennis nodded, "That sounds like Prof. Herd."

"What grade did you get in his class?"

"Oh, I got an A minus. But he was kind of generous, trying to keep his classes full. See, logic used to be required, but then Saint Johns got a bunch of computers and media equipment so people can choose between something like Technology 101 or logic; and of course most students choose to watch TV and movies and play with computers."

"So they can do essays on bad versions of Shakespeare, right? That's what we did at the U of I."

"Pretty much. I think that's why he took early retirement: not enough pretty girls in his classes, just some earnest students who wanted to be the next Sartre."

"Is that why you took it?"

"Not really," Dennis said. "I did it to learn to think for myself and mess with the minds of those trying to mess with mine; like the subliminal message people. I mean, Irving's right: a person can build a popular cult around himself." He nibbled a moment, then added, "Or herself."

"And that's what you want?"

"Maybe. Did you see that show on Shakespeare last week?"

"No. When was it on?"

"Thursday, I think. It was interesting. Some scholar had a theory that Shakespeare retired early so as to work on the King James' translation of the *Bible*. Only since none of the poets would get credit for translating it, hence the title *King James*, Shakespeare worked variations of his name into the parts he translated; something like: 'I have the will to shake spear.'"

"Wouldn't that be considered blasphemous? A Shakespeare version of the *Bible*? That sounds like self-worship."

"She didn't talk about that, though I'm sure there'd be people who would think so. Personally, I think he was just having a little fun and signing his autograph. Who knows? Maybe he had a vision from God telling him to do it."

Bernadette asked, "Isn't that what you and Irving complain about with popular cults?"

"True. However, like Captain Pirate, Shakespeare was a master at it."

"Well, I don't see the difference. It sounds like hypocrisy to me."

"That's because you have these. You're a natural born cult figure. We peons have to really work to get what we want."

"Oh," Bernadette said, "oh, and I don't have to put up with all the cut-backs in welfare down at Human Services? Do you know how hard it is to tell someone they don't qualify because the county doesn't have the funding?"

"I forgot about that. How many more years do you have left in school?"

"Two, if I want to be a social worker. Most of my credits will transfer to Saint Johns. But I think I'll change my major."

"What to?"

"I'm not sure yet. That's why I've been studying the class' catalogue."

"At least I got the woodpile full while you were thinking it over."

"Maybe I'll be a psychiatrist. That way, when you mess up people's minds, I can help straighten them out."

"Or at least give them pills to sedate them into not noticing how we're manipulating them."

"Can you be any more cynical?"

"I could try," Dennis said. "You know, that used to be a school of thought-training: how to be a cynic."

"What happened? Did they all drop-out because they got enough education to be cynical about cynicism?"

Dennis laughed, "Sounds like a reasonable explanation. Then they turned to irony so as to laugh about things like George Bush Junior being an Ivy League scholar who talks like a drunken pig-farmer. Only a true cynic realizes that the joke is on them."

"He does sort of remind me of a Shakespeare clown who misuses words and meanings. Only Shakespeare made sure to keep the hierarchy of speech consistent with the status of the roles. He would've been so confused by Bush, he wouldn't know what to write."

"Oh, Shakespeare would've worked for him all right. He just would've found subtle ways of ridiculing him. It was either that or off with his head."

"That's not something we have to worry about."

"Come on, Bernadette; you were the one saying Washington D.C. sent an agent to spy on you at work."

"Well, they did. She had a real harmless quality to her, but I caught her hunting through the files to make sure we cut back on food stamps and county assistance. Since when does the federal government have jurisdiction over how the county spends money?"

"That's when you decided to go back to school, right?"

"Yeah," Bernadette said. "She made me more paranoid than Captain Pirate. I guess what bothers me most is she can always say she was just following orders."

"Do you remember what Bill Clinton said when asked what his new covert agency would do?"

"No."

"He said he couldn't tell because it's a secret."

"Oh, that is funny."

"See," Dennis said, "those agents are supposedly following orders, but of course they also have their own agendas. Some might be or seem harmless; others are really after personal power over the lumpem."

"Guardian angels gone astray, eh?"

"With the magic of technology. I really get a kick out of movies about techno-guardian angels freeing humanity from technology gone bad. I mean, they spend millions of dollars on the special effects to herd people into a theater where they get hypnotized by subliminal messages."

"Yeah; and you guys go see every single one of them."

"Like I say, they're funny."

"Isn't the real irony that you spend money on them?"

"Ooooh. Good point. I hate it when you're right about stuff like that."

"As Irving would say, sometimes we all need a kick in the ass to get us out of our clouds of self-worship."

"Or as you would say: 'Don't be such an ass.'"

"Do I say it that often?"

"It started out as Jackass; you gradually shortened it."

"I guess we all have our little spells or incantations, limited only by vocabulary."

"And look who are chief is," Dennis brayed. "I had a Classics' class sophomore year and the prof. said in ancient times the royal courts would take on the affectations of the residing chief: if they lisped or stuttered, everybody else would too."

"Oh, great," Bernadette said; "so everyone will soon be talking like drunken pig-farmers. Good thing you guys already have a start."

"I haven't played the tough cowboy role in a while, Bernadette. Irving might do it on occasion, but I don't."

"He'd get real mad about us making fun of Bush," she said; "then he'd complain about what a moron he is."

"Irving's more into duality than we are. I mean, he has a hard time dividing his loyalties, but when he does, he goes all the way."

"I never thought I'd hear him laugh about being called a nigger. But he sure has a thing for black women."

"Oh yeah. He'll sit and watch them play basketball while everyone bitches to turn it off. He was bummed that he missed Captain Pirate come on the air as an Amazon."

Bernadette said, "He complained about all the blacks moving to Demosberg, but after rugby matches with Holy Trinity he goes to strip-bars to check them out."

"Who told you that? Celeste?"

"She's the one who said I should have him tested for diseases."

"Well, I don't think he slept with any of them, but I didn't hang around to find out. I'm kind of surprised he didn't punch me for telling Celeste. So what happened?"

"I don't want to talk about it; you guys already know too much as it is."

"Well, we're about out of time. They'll be waiting for us at the cabin."

*** *** ***

The four stopped at a grocery store on their way back to the tavern to pick up some appetizers for the pheasant and duck Irving had shot. He cleaned and dressed the birds while Celeste finished cleaning the bar. Dennis and Bernadette watched cartoons. They sat down to eat at the table the young woman had been posed on, Irving flicking the channel to an international news station.

Irving told Celeste that he had talked to an insurance agent who offered a packaged deal for the tavern workers. "When you fill out the forms," Irving said, "don't tell them you smoke. I'm not positive, but they'd probably raise the premium."

The TV screen, split in half showing tapes of George Bush Junior and Osama Bin Laden in what looked like a vehement debate, flickered and a moment of suspense kept the utensils halfway from plates to mouths. A man appeared in clergy black: suit, tie, and hat. A young Indian boy was hanging on to the preacher's elbow as he sang:

"Leaning, leaning…Leaning on the arm of God."

2.

Top Heavy

I've gotten to a stage of life where memories have become as important as the present; and, just as the Muses were once key factors for humans who sought enlightenment, so do females have similar roles as keepers of my memories. My ex-wife does not understand it, but I try not to be too hard on her because former girlfriends from thirty or forty years ago don't understand it either; perhaps I should have my phone disconnected to keep from calling on them.

To live in the present can be a strange and terrible thing. I recently went to a tavern I infrequently visit to see a young lady who reminds me of a high school girl I had a brief fling with when I was 17. The young lady I'd gone to see had cut off all her hair and her shirt hung limply down the front. I almost cried. However, she was polite and consoling, so I finished my beer and left. When I got home, I was tempted to click on the porno cable channel to see if my favorite matronly star was performing. Instead, I languidly re-read Gulliver's travels to Laptua.

There is something heartening about that particular adventure. My favorite part is the large-headed men who are struck with blown-up bladders on sticks to keep them from digressing. While I was teaching, it was one of my most recurrent digressions, typically while quickly covering Sartre: a thousand pages on the essence of nothing sounds like an essay on digression.

The Hindus make a little more sense out of none sense. Still, their Nirguna Atman does not leave much room for a beatific vision; and the Saguna Atman is essentially male dominated. However, I could be wrong. I once remarked in an Eastern Philosophy class that a Hollywood filmmaker's adventure flick of an archeologist battling for Shiva's sacred stones, set in the first half of the 20th Century, showed the caste system as a form of slavery. A young woman roused up and said the movie was a stupid exercise in exploiting the idea that, despite having leaders like Gandhi and Nehru, the Indian people were incapable of governing themselves without resorting to enslaving through belief. I thanked her for her comments and moved on to Buddhism.

A few years ago, I set about my own translation of Dante's *Divine Comedy* with an Italian to English dictionary. I never got past Virgil to Beatrice. I never made it to Rome or Greece. I've never been out of the United States of America. Once, I was in the running to receive an award I did for a paper covering Plato's humor; the award included an all-expenses paid voyage to Athens. I lost to a humorless Freudian interpretation of Socrates' call to the healer Aesculapius.

Such is the era we live in; and I have tried to adjust. For instance, realizing the limitations of my audience has brought forth metaphors I believe they can understand: Plato's shadows on cavern walls becomes TV or computer screens. More's Utopia is now a rock song about imagining the relinquishing of possessions on a global scale and harmony and peace ensuing from it.

I have to admit I'm not very good at such comparisons, as is obvious by my inadvertent racist comments in Eastern Philosophy. It does not help that I am a reactionary. Some thirty years ago a book swept Saint John's campus. It was written by someone named Kurt Vonnegut, who had the distinction of having spent some time not just in Germany during World War II, but also at a state university's writing program in Iowa. As I droned on about the essence of time being marked by the changes of philosophy, and its interpretations of things like slavery, my students made references to said book. I didn't tell them I hadn't read it and most likely never would, but at least they were interested in something other than protesting required courses in Latin and logic.

I used to call students 'My little noodle-heads' because, like I did when their age, they would vacillate as the courses covered various philosophies. In some of them I could see a physical change: the cynics in their grubby clothes became stoics with austere dress and upright posture. Oh, what fun I had, teasing them and quoting Ovid's *Metamorphoses*. The atmosphere changed again in the 1990s and I was quietly warned not to make deprecating remarks to students, including the F-word: freshman.

It is a wind-swept night in late November in the insipid year of Our Lord 2002. Due to nostalgic reasons, I turned on the TV to watch a Peanuts' special about Thanksgiving.

The Charlie Brown philosophy was a very popular item during the revolutionary 1960s: 'Happiness is a warm blanket,' and so on. For myself, the landlord hasn't turned on the furnace so while I'm not happy wrapped up in my favorite blanky, I am at least comfortable.

Perhaps it is appropriate that American philosophy has been boiled down to comic strips that one can clip out and hang on the refrigerator door to ponder while getting a diet soda. Charlie Brown had his Lucy, Patty, and Marcie; and of course his unnamed beatific vision: the little red-haired girl. At his zenith, Charlie Brown adorned more office doors of professors than Charles Darwin has since he published *Origin of the Species.*

I remember a debate I had with an ABM (Angry Black Man). It was well before someone made a movie of Malcolm X's life to spread his philosophy via baseball caps. It must have been in the early 1970s, before I began inflating grades, for he was vehemently opposed to the D minus I gave him on a paper about Thomas Aquinas. Now that I think about it, I'm certain it was the era of Pat Buchanan writing insane speeches for Richard Nixon; Buchanan was a Seneca who should have been fired and ignored long before he won the vote in our county's primary presidential elections in 1996.

Unfortunately, the conversation with the ABM did not take place behind the blank door to my office; rather, directly following the return of the paper during class.

"What is this?" he asked. "A D minus? Why?"

"We can talk about it later."

"Why not now? I know I'm not the only one unhappy with my grade." A few heads bobbed in tentative agreement. "You see?" he crowed.

"Very well," I said, undiplomatically. "Your paper was nominally about Thomas Aquinas. However, as I recall, you summarily dismissed him in your first paragraph and went on to espouse the virtues of Black Power."

"Well, it's an important philosophy."

"Of that, I do not doubt," I said, changing tactics. "However, you did not choose such to be your paper, nor is it covered in this course."

"Well, it should be."

I smiled, "This is a medieval European philosophy class. Modern philosophy is covered next semester."

"I hope you're not teaching it."

"As a matter of fact, I'm not."

"Good. I'm no Uncle Tom."

I should have let the subject end there; instead, I inquired, "Have you read *Uncle Tom's Cabin*?"

"I don't need to read that trash."

"You evidently feel the same way about Thomas Aquinas."

He said sullenly, "I read him."

"Good. Then I'll be fair and give everyone who didn't like their grades one week to turn in another paper."

Ah, that was the beginning of the end. My despotic rule was over and I knew it. Papers started coming in late, illiterate, or both. Word got around that I was an easy B, so long as papers were done and tests taken. Eventually, it became known that I would give a mark of unfinished before failing anyone.

How different the ABM was from the saucy black lady who enlivened my last logic class. She automatically invented rhyming phrases to my arguments while flashing her sprinter's toned legs to the joy of my heart. She made the ridiculous sublime.

"So you see, 'if' is not a logical way to begin a sentence."

"However, 'but' is okay when not used as nonsense."

I had to stop class a few times to ask her to quiet down; not because I wanted to, rather due to the other students getting visibly upset. Personally, I'd have liked to turn the whole class over to her and sat in the audience. She asked me to work at one of the home track meets as a timer, and gave me a hug when she finished second and qualified for nationals in the 200.

I went into the kitchen and got a bottle of beer. I squeezed a section of lime into it. Chugging it down, I thought: Ah, mother's milk.

I've been thinking of saving my pennies to make a trip to Ireland. I'd like to see the nation of poetic nonsense, though I've never gotten through any of James Joyce's works. Perhaps what I miss most in philosophy are the parables. Modern philosophy is sorely lacking in stories and poetry, having forego them to debate the semantics of every word's meaning.

I recall a young man in the 1980s approaching me after we had covered Boethius, saying a great novel had been written which revolved around his philosophy of Fortune. The young man wrote the title down for me and, since after a few years no one else broached the subject, I decided it might be good enough to read. It was the appropriate novel for the 1980s: filled with every character's grasp for elusive, victorious illusions. It also seemed somehow right that the man who wrote it killed himself before Fortunata had a chance to spin his wheel upward; so went Boethius: perished before published.

A TV program is on about the natural harmonic beauty of Mozart and Beethoven. I feel like flinging the remote control through the screen with an anguished cry, 'Their fathers made them!' But no. No, let the audience think the child Ludwig was never hit for striking the wrong chord.

The vortex of time has caught up with me and I'm spinning in its snares. I light up what my sons call nipples and puff away. I should know by now there are times when I should not read that book. Ah, Fortunata, you wanton slut!

I would quote the *I-Ching* or Lao Tzu, however, that would be hypocritically sententious of me, as I am not very familiar with their philosophies. I do know that a king's ability to change is an important thesis of the works.

I go to my computer and check the singles-in-my-area web site. I delete it and make a down payment for an airline ticket to Dublin.

3.

The Canyon of Temples

Charlie Herd awoke from dreams of erotic statues falling down around him: breasts, heads, and legs shattered in a cacophonous bombardment. A pudendum nearly landed on his upward lifted face.

He consciously rolled off the sofa- which he had not pulled into a bed the night before- enjoying the bump as he landed on the floor. He crawled a few yards, muttering, "Aqua," then stood and walked to his kitchenette where he got a glass of ice water.

Not much of a hangover, he decided: only 10 a.m. and the spittoon cup is empty. He took the beer cans that were upside down in the sink, put them in a plastic grocery bag and tied it in a neat bowknot.

He thought about calling his ex-wife and insisting Junior be ready when Charlie arrived. What would be the point, he thought: I don't want to go either.

He would have time to read and take a nap until 4 p.m. and make it in time to miss his uncle's wake. Charlie considered skipping the entire affair, but knew his car, parked outside his apartment, would be marked by townspeople, and didn't feel like working up a lie about being picked up by a relative. The townsfolk would have already noted his absence at the home high school wrestling match the previous night.

The joys of living in a fish bowl, Charlie thought as he went to his bookshelf to select some material. TV was simply too mind-numbing when he felt the languid layover from a night of beer drinking. He knelt before his books, enjoying the satisfying sound of his knees creaking and popping.

He said softly: "Let's see what we have here. Ah, I've gone through *The Godfather* enough times that I have dreams of being with a Mafioso pornographer. Wish I had some James Bond. Can't believe the library doesn't have any. Probably too busy reading their *Bibles*; think James Bond is bad for morals. Maybe they have a point: that crazy clan that lived across the street from us had two sons named Sean and Ian, both penitentiary bound. God, why did I sell all my Edgar Rice Burroughs? Guess I was embarrassed about being 24 and still having them. What's that book Lois keeps pushing on me? Can't remember. I'll re-read her letter later. *The Pope of Greenwich Village*: the next time I'm in Demosberg, I'll return it; it's only about eight years overdue. I guess I'll settle with *Dune*; it reminds me of the dream I had the other night."

Charlie tossed the book onto his lounge chair and went to the bathroom thinking of his dreams; how he'd been in a spacecraft with family, friends, and various associates. They had been surrounded by other spaceships and were monitoring the destruction of earth. Following the climax of the planet's demise, the spacecrafts were hurled into their preordained heavens. Each ship was equipped with devices that recorded its version of the apocalypse and when the earth simmered down, the spacecrafts rejoined to form a complete recorded whole of the devastation. The more the destruction was viewed and critiqued, the more the instability of the confederacy grew; as if just watching the world's annihilation was enough to relive it. Of course, bickering ensued as the spaceships' inhabitants proclaimed their idiosyncratic versions to be the wholly correct one.

Charlie, named after Darwin, had found himself in the midst of a heated debate over evolution. When he tried to walk out and find a place more suitable for his mental abilities, he found the door barred and was told to return to his seat and take notes.

'You don't understand,' he explained. 'I'm not supposed to be here with these braniacs. I should be with the sports' writers.'

He was led back to his chair, grumbling about fish bowls, and began writing down things he didn't understand in a language that was incomprehensible.

"Karma," Charlie mumbled, finishing his toilet. "Maybe I'd be happier with the Bible-bangers, but my genetic and environmental background has caused me to be raised as a 30-year-old divorced man whose sole belief is reporting the actions of others."

He briefly wondered if his editor would say anything about Charlie missing the wrestling match. He had honestly thought he would go to Stillwater the previous evening, but thoughts of beer and his family had settled the matter.

Well, Charlie thought, I'll just have to cook up a story about picking up Junior and making my ex out to be a bitch. Which won't be hard to do, though I'll have to be careful about exaggerating. Divorce was definitely an anomaly in Triton Valley, and Charlie wanted to draw as little attention to his own as possible; especially since he was dating one of the town's former stars.

Lois Lodge was 10 years his junior. A two-time winner of the class B cross country championship, she had often been featured in Charlie's articles. She was a junior at a college in Demosberg, where she ran both cross country and track; though she was no longer a star, she was still a town favorite. She attended church and social functions, sometimes bringing Charlie along, with a vivacious skill that precluded talk of her being with a divorced older man.

Charlie was endeared to her subtle proposal that more sexual activity would come his way if he chose her best friend's sister, a swimmer who made it to the state finals and finished 4th in the backstroke, as Triton Valley's female athlete of the year. Charlie had indeed chosen the young lady, though he knew he would be overruled by his editor for a senior who won the state title in tennis.

Charlie turned the TV to an all-sports' network, saw they were featuring skate-boarding, and turned the channel to cartoons. He thought: If I'm going to watch the ridiculous, I might as well go all the way.

He settled in his recliner to read about the adventures of Paul Muad'dib, thinking later he might find a news story about the wars; or failing that, something about Israel.

An hour later, Charlie stepped outside to check mail. The balmy December breeze was a pleasant surprise and he thought he would go for a run, only he didn't want to be noticed by the citizens.

"Cowering in my apartment like a scared gopher," he muttered, taking the mail out of his box. "Oh, no! A letter from Everett."

Stanley Everett had been Charlie's dorm partner for three years at Saint Johns College in Stillwater. They had both been English majors: Everett in literature and Charlie in non-fiction writing, with an emphasis in journalism.

Everett was a natural born complainer. Once, he had gone on for what seemed two hours about how their mentors, the professors, took something called the *TLS* out of the periodical room and never returned it.

Everett had said, "They set themselves up as icons to us. Tell us we should read critical studies on books, and they steal the best one from our library! And who's paying for it? We are, that's who. They should get their own subscriptions."

Wearily, Charlie said, "Why don't you tell the dean of academics? I mean, what am I supposed to do about it?"

"Because they'll know it was me and be harder on me grade-wise."

Charlie laughed. "You may have a point there. You can't go about tarnishing their images with accusations of theft without them paying you back one way or another."

"So will you do it?" Everett asked. "You're a model student: they won't suspect you."

"Leave me out of it. I have my own battles to fight."

"Like what?" Everett snorted contemptuously. "Your radio show?"

Charlie nodded, "Don't listen if you don't like it."

The college had a small band radio station that covered the campus and a few surrounding blocks. Charlie had a sports' show twice a week, which he was proud of, and fondly hoped would pad his resume.

"You know," Everett said, "I wasn't going to tell you this but everyone on our floor makes fun of you for trying to imitate those morons on TV."

Charlie blinked, "What do you mean?"

"Oh, you know; like getting all excited and changing your voice to say a play at third base was 'Un-believe-able' when it was pretty routine."

Charlie blinked again, "They make fun of me?"

"Yeah. Haven't you heard them when you walk down the hall? You gotta find some new catchphrases or something. I mean, you use all the same ones as the magazines and TV shows."

"And I thought I was being original."

"Well, you thought wrong."

For his next broadcast, Charlie did his homework; armed with the games from the *Odyssey* and the *Iliad*, he spun metaphor upon simile, using the epics as material. He was disappointed when Everett told him no one had been listening because a fire alarm had cleared the dorm.

After that, Charlie's broadcasts became more home-styled. He interviewed the college's athletes and visiting high school recruits, whom he found to be engagingly self-conscious. Later, when he began working for *The Triton Valley Ledger*, he opened his interviews with the local high school athletes by asking them what was their most memorable sports' moment, personal or as a spectator. He even bought a file cabinet to keep the stories sorted, planning to run a special in the newspaper in fifteen or twenty years on the most popular sports' events as told by the town's youth.

Charlie returned to his seat and opened Everett's letter:

"Hey Fatso, what's up?"

Charlie put the letter aside, then picked it up. As unbearable as Everett could be, he often had insight to the world-at-large. Apparently, he'd just bought a bit of bomber weed and was relaxing from his duty of teaching English Literature at a community college in Sacramento, California.

"What do you think of North Korea being called part of an axis of evil and responding to live up to the slander by tossing out weapons' inspectors so as to restart their nuclear capability? Our president sure goes in for name-calling, doesn't he? I used to do the same thing in about 4th grade until I got punched-out by a big kid I called Ape once too often. The thing is, our country's speakers are picking up on the name-calling; and so are other nations. I suppose if we had literary greats like Shakespeare or Milton inventing poetic diatribes against our nation's foes I would be more willing to listen and pay heed. Oh well, it's hard for writers to compete with the movies' four-letter words, violence, and flag-waving. By the way, forgive me for calling you Fatso; it's a bad habit that I'll blame on George Bush Junior. After all, he's our example."

Everett went on to bash the antics of high-profile athletes then quoted Shelley's *Ozymandias*: "Look on my Works, ye Mighty, and despair!" Charlie finished reading the letter with no plans to write back any time soon. What was there to write? He could brag about Lois; describe his uncle's illness and death; detail his ex-wife's crimes against fatherhood; tell about the bashful farm-boy who had thanked Charlie for his article (which he had exaggerated in his printed interview because the young man had been too quiet to say much other than he liked playing both full-back and linebacker). As for world news, *The Triton Valley Ledger* was serenely isolated from carrying anything other than back-page tiny articles of events outside Blake County. Charlie only watched the national and international cable TV news when stirred to it by dreams or books like *Dune*.

Still, Everett's listing various crimes by famous athletes could not go ignored. Perhaps a response from Charlie telling of the charitable deeds of local athletes was in order: stories of farm-kid stars who helped their neighbors at harvest time; the church groups they belonged to who had food and clothing drives to aid the beleaguered poor of Demosberg, many of whom were black; the literacy and math studies by Lois and her friends to improve the skills of local and Demosberg citizens so they could earn their high school GEDs.

The imperfections were sordid: kids playing baseball kitty with a barn-full of cats; rumors of rapes, molestations, and abortions; vandalism and racism. Why pour fuel on the fire by telling Everett of the town's Laotian family packing up when the daughter supporting her family had been fired, for dubious reasons- which warranted a lawsuit by the young woman- from Triton Valley's locally owned pharmacy?

Charlie got another glass of ice water and wondered about his grandfather's tales of playing ice hockey on the frozen Mississippi River while a youth. Perhaps Charlie could get him to expound on it after the funeral; it might make an interesting paragraph or two for the landlocked Tritons.

As he considered this, Charlie found his mind wandering to the memories of a chesty blonde he had been friendly with at Saint Johns. It was a sunny May afternoon and she was lying on the grassy hillock outside the library with a gal-pal, ostensibly critiquing the scribes of her fiction writing class. Charlie had joined them and read a portion of a story about a young man who cared more about his dog than his girlfriend.

"This is terrible," Charlie exclaimed, the recent about-to-be-proclaimed seminarian.

The young lady rolled over on her belly, leaned on her elbows, and the crevasse of her well-formed breasts showed beneath her halter-top, visually intoxicating Charlie. "You don't like it?"

Charlie tore his gaze away and waved at a few priests who were passing by, watching him guardedly. "No. The characters are so unlikable."

"Don't you think," the other young woman said from where she was basking in the sun in shorts and a t-shirt, "that many people are unlikable?"

"Yeah. But other than putting them in hell or purgatory, why write about them?"

Charlie had just finished Laurence Binyon's translation of Dante's *Divine Comedy* and had eagerly read Ignatius of Loyola's guide to holy visions. The Society of Jesus was a bit too challenging for Charlie, so he settled for the idea of being a parochial priest. Junior year and a busty freshman- no, first-year student- named Rachel, changed his plans.

Charlie leaned back in his recliner, thinking: They're still calling freshmen in high school freshmen; maybe there's hope yet: the patriarchal system can't be all wrong. Feeling hardboiled, he replaced *Dune* on his bookshelf and got his paperback copy of *The Big Sleep*, enjoying the tale of an oil tycoon and his slutty daughters.

After reading Raymond Chandler's story for an hour and a half, Charlie reflected on his own perceptions of guilt. Perhaps, he thought, I've lost my ability to romanticize guilt. The day-to-day drudgery of living with my own banal sins has calloused my desire and imagination for punishing or helping others.

The Triton Valley Ledger had conducted a poll the previous week on the impending war with Iraq. Charlie had answered, over the phone, that he had no opinion and would greatly appreciate his number being removed from the list of future polling.

The questioner had asked, "Don't you believe in freedom for the Iraqi people?"

"Not if it means installing another Shah of Iran and his inheritor the Ayatollah."

"So you don't agree with the president?"

"Not if you're unable to accept statements that qualify my perspective. Just put me down as 'No opinion.'"

"Moral and social commitments," Charlie snorted, putting the book back in its place and getting his copy of *Jaws*. He thought: The closest I've come to being public about such things are the articles I did after the 9-11 air attacks when sporting events were cancelled or postponed. And that was only because I didn't have anything else to write about for a few weeks. I wouldn't want my readers to think I care more about someone's batting average than…what did I call it? The unforgettable day of infamy? Something like that. I used the words tragic and sad about 18 times in two paragraphs before I got out my thesaurus. Actually, I didn't think I had it in me to ponder over so well. Too bad I can't do the same for my uncle. Then again, today is not a command performance.

On such recollection, Charlie was embarrassed to be part of the oozing sympathy of the media on 9-11-01 and was not proud to be able to pull it off. He was particularly shamed by the TV hounds claiming how much they cared about the horrible catastrophe striking others, then zoomed in with replays of people jumping out of the buildings, describing, 'Look at how they're holding hands in their final moments.' Charlie thought: You gotta have a lot of guts to proclaim such sincerity while televising people splattering on the cement. We sure did our share of self-congratulations for being so sensitive.

Charlie settled in to read about the relentless Great White Shark. He had never pretended that reading the novel could take the place of Ahab's pursuit of oil and revenge in *Moby Dick*, as Charlie had substituted other books with remakes and movies. Everett had accused Charlie, on more than one occasion, of being illiterate through choice rather than by breeding or environment; by senior year, they barely talked at all except for trivialities.

One night, when both their girlfriends were busy, Charlie had acquiesced to Everett's offer of sharing a bottle of rum mixed with pineapple juice. About halfway through the bottle, Everett asked, "What happened to you, man?"

"What do you mean?" Charlie asked cautiously.

"You were gonna be a priest-scholar. You read Dante and Milton when you were only a sophomore. Hell, I can't read that stuff. I mean, the only version of Dante I read was some modern crap with Rorschach tests on the covers."

Charlie shrugged, "I guess I got burned out."

"Bullshit, man. It's Rachel. You read the *Iliad* and the *Odyssey* when I was still on *Lord of the Flies*. And now you're reading what? *Lord of the Rings* for the sixth time? You could be a *Bible* scholar if you wanted."

"Well, maybe I don't want it."

"Why not?"

"It doesn't excite me any more."

"Fake it 'til you make it, man. I'm not saying get excited over every piece of literature, but if you keep reading, eventually it'll sink in and get the cogs going."

Charlie shook his head, "It doesn't feel worth it any more."

"Why not?"

"According to my brother, who likes quoting Ken Kesey, the art of writing- and hence, reading- is dead."

"You're gonna take some acid freak's word for it?" Everett exclaimed. "That's like believing God is dead because some opium addict says so."

"I'm not that stupid, Stan; I'm just giving you someone's point of view."

"What's your own view then?"

"I'm not sure; but I do know Homer isn't exactly a common standard any more. He's like Latin in the Catholic Church."

There was a knock on the door and Everett let Rachel in. "Hi guys. Oh, you're getting drunk."

"Not really," Charlie lied adroitly. "Mostly we're just talking."

Rachel sat on Charlie's bed and asked, "What about?"

"Homer, of all things," Charlie said.

"What about him?"

"Have you read Homer?" Everett asked, barely managing to keep the sneer off his face.

"Part of the *Iliad*," Rachel replied. "World Lit."

"Didn't like it, huh?" Charlie asked.

"Too male dominated; even the teacher thought so."

Everett said, "Don't tell me: it was Bickle, right?"

"No, as a matter of fact it was Scaley."

Everett snorted, "It figures. He wants to keep his classes full with chicks."

"There were plenty of goddesses and women in the *Iliad*," Charlie said.

"They were all manipulative bitches," Rachel responded.

"So?" Charlie said, "I mean, Homer didn't exactly have the men be any better."

"You are getting drunk."

"No I'm not. It just seems to me that Homer was honest- in his own visionary way- about war and sex. For instance, Bickle always bashing men as evil could serve as a model for one of the goddesses being furious about not getting her way."

"That's pretty good, Charlie," Everett said. "A goddess of Sappho while we're at it."

"That, I don't want to think about."

"Just because she doesn't teach the common patriarchal authority figure way doesn't mean she's a lesbian."

Charlie replied, "It doesn't make her open-minded or very imaginative either."

"Well, you're drunk. I'm leaving."

"Okay. I'll call you tomorrow."

*** *** ***

Charlie dozed, remembering Everett's applause when Rachel was safely out of earshot. The ringing phone startled him and he sat up, thinking it was his alarm clock. He picked up the receiver, after getting his bearings, and it was Rachel calling to apologize about Junior not wanting to attend the funeral. They made small talk about Charlie's plans to drive to Stillwater, and amicably said their goodbyes.

Charlie patted his belly and went through his routine of calisthenics. That task completed, he fried some eggs and made toast. He ate in his recliner, flicking through the cable channels, not paying much attention to the screen; it was merely a blocker to the rest of that night Everett and he spent talking of various, drunken things.

*** *** ***

"You remind me of that poem by Browning," Everett said.

"*Fra Lippo Lippi*?"

"Is that the one about the painter who had the skills and talent to be great, but ended up mediocre because he only painted his wife?"

"I don't remember. I think it's the one about the painter living in a monastery, but goes out tom-catting in the red-light district. Which is probably how I'd end up if I wasn't marrying Rachel."

Everett laughed, "I could see you doing that."

"Then why do you think I've chosen what I have?"

"I just don't like seeing potential greatness settling for the mundane."

"That's the way the world is, Stan. Nobody cares about the games in Homer; they will, however- as I know from firsthand experience- imitate all the jock-talkers and magazine writers."

"It sounds like devolution."

"No; it's what my father would call artificial selection."

"Why did he name you after Darwin? I mean, he teaches philosophy for chrissake."

"He wanted me to be a biologist. I sure showed him, huh?"

"Really? You never told me that."

"Yeah. When he and my mom were arguing, I'd just go up to my room and read sports' magazines. I couldn't really concentrate on anything else because the tension was too high. Luckily, about the time they decided to divorce, I was old enough for college and didn't have to choose between them. It really messed up my little brother though. He became their ping-pong ball."

"That's why you read like a fiend the first couple years of college: finally got some peace and quiet."

Charlie laughed, "There's probably a lot of truth in that. I remember getting hold of Dante and thinking: Some day I'm going to write like him."

"And now you think there's no audience for it."

Charlie shrugged. "Oh, there might be. I just don't want to start putting people like Ronald Reagan in hell. It's too much work and I don't care as much about politics as Milton or Dante. I could do a paper on Joseph Conrad using Marlowe as the name of a Faustian dealer; and Raymond Chandler doing the same; but who cares about Christopher Marlowe's play of selling one's soul? Or Milton's idea of free will and the loss of Eden? What's the good of backing someone like Cromwell as he goes about butchering the Irish?"

"Maybe you could find a hero more suitable."

"Take it from someone who's had more than his share of media and journalism classes: you'll find out details that are repugnant. It's what I like about Homer: all their glaring faults were simply part of the story. Now, either the glaring flaws are the story, or they get ignored altogether. Or better still, the media covers itself in how it handles the story."

"Yeah, they sure like talking about themselves," Everett said. "But then why not teach that?"

Charlie smiled, "The logic of watching TV, eh?"

"I guess you're right, " Everett agreed. "It sounds more mediocre than interviewing a high school linebacker."

"Judgment is different from discrimination," Charlie said. "I remember my dad reading us the *Bhagavad-Gita* after dinner when I was in high school. He put a real emphasis on us developing discrimination instead of judgment. Probably because he didn't want us to be judgmental about the living hell he put my mom through."

"I haven't read that."

"I've got a copy here. He teaches it in one of his philosophy classes, but I think he doesn't understand it. You can have it."

"What's it about?"

"Oh, doing one's duty. To my father, Krishna is sort of a watered-down Christ; instead of carrying one's cross, one carries on their duty to support the caste system. He misses the subtlety of the lower being reincarnated to higher castes as they so deserve."

"Reincarnation? Sounds cool."

"Yeah," Charlie said. "Who knows? Maybe in a previous life I was one of the scribes who helped compose Homer's games. When Judgment Day does arrive, I'll have done my duty with discrimination."

Everett laughed, "But not judgment."

"Like I said, I'm not poetically political enough to put people in hell."

"Not even someone like Bickle who judges people based on their gender?"

"Especially people like her. I'd just as soon avoid that type altogether."

"Do you think there'll be a Judgment Day?"

Charlie laughed and Everett said, "No, I'm serious now. Do you really think there'll be one?"

"We live in perpetual judgment by the powers-that-be so my answer is there'll at least be a perception of a Judgment Day."

"Like, on a bigger scale, right?"

"Yeah," Charlie said. "And if I do my duty in high school sports with discrimination, then I can move on to something higher."

"Like composing part of an epic of the games in heaven?"

"Sounds good to me."

"Well. You got it all figured out."

"Hardly. I just know what I want to spend my time doing. I mean, you want a revolution and I don't."

"Well, it would make things exciting; you have to admit that."

"Right," Charlie said. "Dante and Milton were part of revolutions, and I have to admit I find it very rousing to think the same might happen in America. However, I probably wouldn't take sides because all of them would be extreme. I mean, the last revolution America went through replaced logic with computers, as my father so bemoans. I'm not being judgmental about it, simply using discrimination."

"Well, if I were you I'd want to be like Dante or Milton: think about how great that would be."

"Oh yeah? Think about Saint John exiled to an island, preaching to crabs and fish in between scribbling nonsense about revelations that might be great poetry but damn near impossible to understand unless you actually pray to have it enacted. Myself, the only visions I want to have are from the very thing I ridicule: TV."

"That does seem to be how revolutionary poets end up, doesn't it?"

Charlie nodded. "Milton was lucky: his revolution was considered a success. He sort of reminds me of John the Baptist in reverse: instead of being a poetical prophet who lost his head on a king's whim, he was one of Cromwell's scribes for lopping off the king's noggin."

"Like he was reincarnated from John the Baptist to John Milton?"

"Karma balancing itself. In some ways, John the Baptist was more political than Jesus."

"Who would Jesus be reincarnated as?"

Charlie laughed, "James Joyce: overly fond of word-games wrapped up in stories that are apolitical."

Everett grinned, "The daily grind of epic living. With God his Father as the Judge of all stories."

"The Supreme Artist."

*** *** ***

Charlie rose from the recliner and went to his desk to reread Lois's letter, which finished with a poem she had written for a class:

Icons and Idols

I see the things I desire to see,
sometimes shaded footsteps following me.
I enjoy naked statues of great men,
and paintings of various women
posing as the haloed Virgin Mother.
I also have visions of another
life where I destroy what is most sacred:
where smoke and fire fill caverns with acrid
stench of the painful loss and greatest grief:
then I repent and find Holy Relief.

4.

Memory Killer

I was going through some old files, cases long closed and considered rubbish. I wasn't feeling very nostalgic, however, it was amusing to view my life's work in raw detail. I was looking at the climax of my craft, a photograph of an outstanding member of Parliament in the clutches of a catamite, when there was a tap at my door.

I called, "Come in." I figured it was my secretary about to bother me over severance pay. Instead, a man in a custom-fitted three-piece suit walked in and stood silently in the doorway.

"Mr. Driver?" he asked.

"Yes," I said, switching to English.

"Are you indisposed at the moment?"

"You don't look like a creditor," I said, closing the file and throwing it on the shredder pile. "Come in."

He shut the door behind him and sat in the chair across from my desk. "What a relief to find you here. From what I've heard..." He gave a small shrug.

"If it's a business matter then you should know, from what you've heard, I'm no longer available for services."

"But surely it wouldn't hurt to listen."

"I have a week to leave the country, Mr..."

"Venow. K.P. Venow."

"So I can listen and that's about all I can do."

"If things work out as I hope, Mr. Driver, you may be able to stay as long as you like."

"Oh no. Not another government case."

"No," he assured me. "Something quite different. Something that calls for someone of your exceptional talent and confidence." He paused and when I stayed quiet he went on. "The confidence, I feel certain of; after all, you took the rap as it were for that scandalous affair the tabloids have so loved, without naming your client."

"Yes. Well, as sophisticated as the French like to think they are about sex, the gritty details seem quite upsetting to them."

"Especially when placed in the context of armament secrets being shared in bed."

I said, "That was only an excuse to slime themselves with the muck of other people's private lives."

"Mmm. An interesting insight. But tell me, are you taken with the idea of returning to your trade here in Marseilles?"

"I might be."

"Well then, we'd best get down to business, for time is running low. Have you heard of Comptrollers Inc?"

"It's some new line of computers," I said; "but I only know what I've read in the headlines."

"No doubt next to your own headlines," he said, and I graciously inclined my head. "We have a new model coming out this week, only there are a few problems that stand in the way of truly revolutionizing the world's idea of software." He paused. "Personal matters that have to be attended to." He took an envelope from his suit pocket and removed a piece of paper, which he laid on the desk before me. It was a picture of a voluptuous dark-haired young woman who smiled with insouciant mockery at the camera. "That is my wife, Kelly Giroud-Venow. I want you to kill her memory in me."

I laughed. "Oh, Mr. Venow, thank you for brightening my day."

He looked flustered, "I was given to understand that you have special skills, Mr. Driver, which this case calls for."

I shook my head. "Parlor tricks. A treat I throw in for the gullible. Once, I had a woman in here whose husband died. She missed him and I told her he'd been reincarnated as a parrot. So she went searching through the pet shops until she found one she thought looked like him."

"You're a fake?"

I shook my head again. "They've never been happier. The last I heard, she was teaching it to sing their song."

"But the information I had..."

"Look. Even if I could destroy your memory of her, that would leave a large hole in your consciousness."

"She can be replaced," he said, putting a snapshot of a willowy blonde on top of Mrs. Giraud-Venow.

"Your lover?"

"That's personal."

"Before I'd even begin to consider taking the case I'd want all the facts. I'm not going to plunge into the consciousness of others without knowing what I'm getting into."

He loosened his tie a bit, shifting around uneasily. "It's not a very easy thing to talk about, Mr. Driver. There are certain delicacies..."

"Right. So you haven't been able to make it with her because of your wife."

"She haunts my every thought."

"Tried any medication?"

"I told you: I have a business to run and I can't be doped up."

"Hypnotism?"

He said, "I'm afraid trade secrets might inadvertently come out while I'm under."

"But you think I can just kill a memory and replace it with another."

"It's worse than a terrible song running in your mind that you can't get rid of."

I shook my head, but when he laid a personal check for five-hundred-thousand Euros I became more interested. I made notes while he gave me particulars about the case: birth dates, addresses, religious beliefs. Myself, I'm a 6'2" 200 pound frog-baiting mongrel. My mother taught Scandinavian culture at the University of Marseilles while my father, a Hindu Indian, ran a chain of grocery stores; that is, until they died in a boating accident, which left me with what Venow called exceptional talent. Surviving a 300,000 volt jolt of lightning can do that to some people.

At the end of the interview, Venow left with the two goons who had been waiting in the reception area. Being on his expense tab, I thought I'd go for lunch at the Canabrie. I walked past the spiritualists' shops where they specialized in filling old socks with dirt from the backyard and selling them as energy tokens.

According to the world news, frog-bashing is very en vogue in America; so, not wishing to miss out on a trend, I sat down at one of the pricier outdoor cafes and ordered Freedom Fries and a peanut butter and jelly sandwich. When lunch arrived, I smashed the sandwich on the table and said, "I ordered chunky peanut butter, you dumb frog." I paid and left, taking the receipt to put on Venow's tab.

I thought about calling my wife, but figured she wouldn't take be able to take the bottle out of her mouth long enough to have an intelligible conversation. We had met at a small college in Stillwater, Iowa when we were foreign exchange students. She had taken the news of our exile with the typical grace of a vindictive frog, staying in a blackout drunk on wine and leaving it to me to do the packing. Venow's influence with authorities would probably save what was left of my marriage.

I found Nina in the park being lazily hustled by some old men. "Let's take a walk," I said, and she latched onto my arm. She had been a much sought after medium until she went into a business which she thought of as more honest.

"I've got an interesting case," I said. "Some guy wants a memory killed and replaced by a woman who looks like you. I thought you might be able to help me out."

"Sounds like a nut-job."

"He pays well; and I'm willing to double your fees as both a medium and pro."

I showed her a picture of Karen, the woman Venow wanted as a replacement for his wife. Nina laughed, "My long lost twin sister."

"Amazing, isn't it? Here's the woman he wants omitted."

"She's African?"

"Part. Shall we get a hotel room?"

"We can go under that tree. Say, does this have anything to do with the TPCs?"

"TPCs?"

"Telepathic Computers," Nina said. "Don't you read the newspapers or watch TV?"

"I've been kind of busy."

"It's a new software design. It was supposed to be introduced last week, but some government officials said they were going to investigate it because there seemed to be a problem with users short-circuiting their brains."

"Is that right?"

"Yeah," she said; "but the next day, they said there was no reason to investigate."

"A few payoffs. But thanks for the warning; I'll be sure not to use them. I've had my fill of fooling around with electricity."

We went under the tree and undressed. I assumed the lotus position and she straddled me. We hummed together for a few moments of pleasure and then began concentrating on Venow's case. Abruptly, we were in an astral plane of copulating bodies and Kelly Giroud-Venow appeared as the form Gaia must have looked to Saturn. She laughed at us and plunged her hand into Nina's head. We were back at the park and Nina fell off me, blood streaming from her nose and ears. She mumbled, "Am I a goddess?" as I tried to form astral weapons to protect us.

I could see Kelly Giroud-Venow hovering above us, then she laughed again and vanished.

I got our clothes back on and led Nina, who tottered on her legs like a newborn colt, to the nearest hotel. I put her to bed and stood on the balcony watching the sky grow dark. I noticed something very peculiar and realized the electricity was not working; not a single light was on, as far as I could see, in Marseilles. I watched the traffic jams as cars began to sputter and expire.

Nina was still unconscious, but her breathing was steady. I walked down to the lobby and recognized Venow's goon squad hassling the clerk, who was arguing with them by the glow of a candle.

"No," he said adamantly; "no patrons until the power is back on."

A .38 Smith and Wesson pointed at his face changed his tune. Not wasting time on niceties I surreptitiously crept up behind the gunman, broke his neck, and shattered the kneecap of his pal. I took their guns and spare ammo while the clerk profusely thanked me. He followed me to the front doors, talking of looters and his retirement package, and I went out into the roiling mob.

I was about halfway to Kelly Giroud-Venow's hotel address when I heard a magnificent din approaching. An old man in a second story apartment called down to me, "Come in! Come in or you'll be crushed!"

He was right. We watched an ocean wave of humanity pour down the street, smashing up everything in sight. I thanked him and left, skirting the flames that had been set to cars, trash, and various desiderata which could burn.

I was surprised that there were no armed guards in the lobby, and more than surprised that she answered her door as if expecting me, inviting me into her suite where the electricity was working. She was wearing a dark green skirt and a tight white blouse.

I looked around and saw a computer glowing on the desk. "So what's the story?" I asked. "Some new satellite and software designed to bring about the apocalypse?"

"Gods of a new age," she said, smiling brightly; "and he was going to cheat me of it. Perhaps you've heard the Hindu stories of ascetics rising above their system and enslaving gods; that's what my husband would have done. I don't know how you've managed to get this far, but just being here shows you've got what it takes to help me bring in a new dawn for humanity."

I was not going to give away what I believed was the cause for escaping with my synapses intact: the lightning bolt from childhood that had fried my parents to cinders.

I put my hand in my jacket pocket, hefting the weight of the pistol, "For thine is the kingdom."

"Indeed."

"You just hurt a friend of mine."

"Karmic justice," she said. "One shouldn't take vows of fidelity and then break them so easily."

"What's my punishment?"

"Oh, I'll think of something fitting. Meanwhile, let's talk about rewards."

"Ah. Now we're getting somewhere."

"Yes, I thought you'd feel that way."

"And now it's time to take them." I leveled the gun at her, walked over to the computer and clicked out the diskette. "Your greatness would be even more brilliant if you served it with distinguished morality."

"You poor, moronic bastard," she said. "Do you really think I haven't made copies?"

"You're wrong."

"Oh? Am I now?"

I said, "I do know who my parents are."

I stole a sailboat and made it across the Mediterranean to the Suez Canal. From there, I was able to get aboard a cargo ship bound for India. I heard news that Marseilles was quarantined, but that similar outbreaks had occurred throughout France.

Fortunately, I had my passport and was able to catch a flight to New Delhi. I used the diskette at my uncle's estate to pinpoint where I wanted to go: a cavern amongst the Himalayas. My uncle made some phone calls and managed to get me connected to a climbing expedition that didn't care if I went blundering about the mountains on my own, so long as I didn't take any of their provisions.

I was met in the foyer by Ganesha, who told me to sit on a rock and wait, for his parents were busy resting. As I sat there, I read a parchment Ganesh handed me entitled *The Bardo News*. A nameless warrior was described as rampaging around the world, bringing death and destruction as he blindly sought to mate with his mother. I'll say one thing for the Hindus: any religion that has an elephant-headed god, Ganesha, as chief scribe knows how to laugh at itself.

Eventually, Ganesh showed me to the interior of the cavern, where plants grew to the light of a disk on the ceiling. Shiva and Uma were bickering over a plant that he said was not ready to be made into Soma. They quarreled, kissed, and argued some more.

Ganesha watched them with a smile, then announced me, after Shiva relented and Uma clipped the buds from the plant. Shiva was expansive, hugging me to his bosom, while Uma was somber and withdrawn.

She sighed, "I really thought the earth had more time."

"Now, dear, we've been planning this for eons," Shiva said. "We can make our final move to the Andes."

I asked, "You're leaving the Himalayas?"

Shiva nodded, "Every two-bit explorer with money to burn has come to knock about our home. We kill a few off, but still, there's just no peace and quiet like there used to be."

"And they seem to think we owe them something," Uma said.

"Well, he's here now. They'll have to make do with him."

"Me?" I asked.

"Why, yes. Didn't Ganesh show you the old copy of *The Bardo News* from when you were a child? Before the boating incident?"

"You killed my parents?"

"Oh no," Shiva said; then corrected himself, "Well, technically yes. However, we're your parents. You see, you were coming of an age when an incestuous mess had to be avoided. And now that Kali is in possession of the TPCs, the rest of the story can unfold."

"Yes, Skanda," Uma said, finally hugging me. "It's your era now: the god of war."

5.

Fallen is Babylon

As Lester Herd drove his delivery truck, he subconsciously hummed a tune. He made his next stop at a place that sold balloons and other party paraphernalia. He often wondered how they could stay in business in Demosberg's crippled economy; however, the town was fond of parades and Lester assumed Party A Go-Go supplied the fete revelers with the necessary supplies. Soon, he thought, there might be parades galore for the returning military.

Lester drove to the shipping depot, unloaded his undelivered packages, turned in his forms, and drove the twenty miles to his house in Stillwater. He made up a little song to pass the time, "Didja see that? Yes, I saw that. A tiny black cat just crossed my path. Singing songs of rapture hoping God will capture my soul and put it in his bowl." He tapped the steering wheel to keep beat and wondered if he was seeing things, or was it just the sunlight reflecting off his windshield?

Carol was in their bedroom sorting laundry. They kissed briefly and Lester put away his clothes, which she had folded. He noticed a full overnight bag and asked, "You're really going through with it?"

"We're staying at the Davidsons' so don't complain about hotel money."

"It's not about money. I just don't see why she can't go alone."

"Moral support, Les."

"To audition for a reality TV show?" he asked.

"She's afraid she might get camera-shy."

"Oh, that'll be a sign of the apocalypse. You know, I took an inventory of the photos on our wall downstairs and she's in more pictures than I am."

"That sounds like you, Les: counting up pictures of people. Why don't you try reading a book?"

"I've read them all. It's a dead and buried art."

She held up her arms as if to ward off an attack, "Don't start quoting Ken Kesey at me. Please."

Lester walked to the bathroom, pondering a new tact, then went downstairs to get a glass of grape juice. Sipping it slowly, he walked to the front room and sat down to play a few games of solitaire.

Twenty minutes later he said, "Ha! Won again," as Carol came downstairs carrying her travel bag.

"Are you leaving already?"

"Yeah. Justine gets off work at 5:30." She kissed him on the cheek and said, "There's some stew in the crock-pot. Don't forget to put the rest in the fridge."

"I was wondering what that smell is."

"I'll see you tomorrow night, unless she gets called back for a second audition. I'll call when we know."

"They're going to decide in one day? Nothing like thinking it over."

"I told you they're on a shoe-string budget. I don't think we even get the cable channel it's on."

"Ah, good news at last. Well, goodbye. Don't want to keep the star waiting."

"Bye."

Lester watched her lights' trail go to the door and rubbed his eyes. "Box Fever," he muttered, diagnosing his visions as being caused by looking at too many packages in the rear of the truck. He wondered why he was getting it so frequently of late; typically, it only occurred during Christmas rush.

When Lester had jokingly described his case of Box Fever to a coworker, Casey had replied, "Maybe it's the rapture calling you."

"Oh, that's right. I forgot you're Pentecostal."

"Would you be interested in joining me at church service?"

"Well," Lester said, "I don't really speak in tongues or anything."

"That's not required. You can just come and sit in and pray and sing."

"Rapture, huh? I never really thought about that. But maybe it's something simpler." Lester laughed uneasily, "Like I'm having a nervous breakdown."

"My minister says the age of the apocalypse is unfolding as it's written in the *Bible*."

"Is that so?"

"He said the defeat of Saddam Hussein is foretold in *Revelation* where John wrote that Babylon is conquered."

Lester said, "I thought Babylon was where Iran is."

"No, it's Iraq. You can talk to my minister about it. He knows how to explain things better. He'd be interested in hearing about your visions."

"Really? Most people get bored talking about that stuff."

"They don't believe in the God of revelations."

"Well," Lester said hesitatingly, "I'm Catholic, but I'll keep it in mind."

"Oh, the Roman Catholic Church fell for the very temptations that Jesus spurned in the desert."

"I never thought about that. But you know, it's kind of weird when you think about it because Jesus also fell for the temptations in a way."

"How?" Casey replied sharply.

"Well, instead of turning stones into bread, he turned his body into bread. And he did promise to make a great empire on earth with Peter as his cornerstone. What was the other one?"

"To fly off the temple and be saved."

"Oh yeah. Well, according to my religion he did ascend bodily into heaven, which is kind of like flying."

Casey shook his head, "That's the wrong interpretation to justify the Catholics' empire. It makes it sound as if Jesus made a deal with Satan."

"That would be one way of dividing the holy and the righteous from the unholy and evil."

"You should come to our Bible-study group. I think our minister could really help you."

"I'll think about it."

Lester sat pondering: Could Lucifer actually be Jesus Christ, making his payment on the cross for having dared to assume he and only he was the way to God?

He said aloud, "Oh, if only my dad hadn't been a philosopher; I really don't need to think of such things. I mean, what next? Is Krishna going to show up and start dancing while playing his flute?"

He moved the TV tray from in front of his chair and began pacing the room, thinking: If I were on some kind of drug it wouldn't be so bad cuz then I'd just tell myself: Well, of course you're seeing things. You're bombed to the gills. But this. Seeing bears and eagles and cats. I can't take much more. It's wearing out my cogs. And when I ask when it will end, it just gets worse. They're even blocking out Carol. What's a guy to do? I'm too scared to even have a beer.

Carol had knitted a quilt, and he took it off the back of the sofa and placed it over the screen of the TV. God, he thought: they're trying to get into my head.

He paced some more, laughing at the cub jaguar that was following him. He wrung his hands and prayed for deliverance. He cursed a string of foul oaths. He thought of old friends he no longer associated with because Carol didn't approve of them. He thought of calling his brother, but instead sat down and watched little Natalie walk over to him and begin taking shards of light from his head and give them to a dark form, which he could only think of as evil death. He thought: Oh, but I don't want to go to hell. Please, Natalie, you can save me. The leukemia only corrupted your body, not your soul. Please sit down and tell me what to do.

She stood looking at him thoughtfully for a moment, no longer pulling parts of him into darkness; then she slowly faded away.

Wait! Don't go! Oh, please don't leave.

He closed his eyes and felt a pain in his ass: I'm in hell and being given the shaft. He cocked his hip and broke wind. Feeling better now, he thought: Just keep it together. Laughed: Saved by a fart.

He opened his eyes and watched a lion roam by. He thought: Now if I could just get it to lie down with a lamb.

None was forthcoming and Lester watched the lion disappear into a wall that a bird flew out of and vanished halfway across the room.

Help, he thought: I need help. Please. Natalie. Oh, please. I need...

He saw above him streets running with milk and remembered reading *Revelation*, thinking: Breasts...statues of breasts to be nursed into the Golden Age image of God.

But I don't want to be perfectly formed. I like who I am because I am. Oh God Natalie preserve me!

The visions faded into lingering swirls and Lester sat down, pulled the TV tray close and continued playing solitaire. He ignored a male's call, "Mother Earth is dying and I cannot suckle her into new life!"

Eventually, he heard music; to be sure, not Beethoven or Mozart, whom he listened to each morning and afternoon during the drive to and from Demosberg. Rather, it seemed highly original rock music: as if the best of the dead and still living artists of the 1960s were putting on a show. Charlie noted a few absentees and encouraged them to partake; then laughed at the egos involved and let the sound continue.

For a moment he watched an old lady Tai Chi on the wall, then he laid his cards out, thinking: The martial arts faded in America with the Vietnam glow.

He pulled at his Fu-Manchu beard and thought: The Mongols had the biggest land empire ever; now they've returned to homesteading. Lester laughed: The horsemen of the apocalypse were simple natives on the nether-ends of the earth. Would they trade their ponies for tanks?

Not our style, an angry flourish of visions and voices told Lester, as a spinning multi-armed figure whacked its way across the room.

Genghis, Lester thought: Gang us…Ganges…Ganesha…

He sat bolt upright, thinking: They're trying to mob me up. Put me in a gang to make us mop each other up. I'll show them and that little bastard, Ganesh.

Lester took the envelope from a charity society in India which he and Carol had requested in thoughts of paying for the raising of an urchin; took it, ripped it in two, and threw the pieces in the kitchen garbage.

"No more visions from famished countries," Lester said aloud, walking back to his seat. "If Carol wants to see them, I'll just find something else to do. I'll no more be ganged up with an organization for the poor than I'd enlist or allow myself to be drafted into the military. Maybe I shouldn't commit euthanasia on a youth in Asia but…"

Thank you, Natalie, for holding my seat.

She touched his face a moment: Yes, just Box Fever.

Oh, she misses the pain.

The punch in the face by the school bully when Lester's older brother was pushed out of place while lining up after recess. Lester tried to intervene and both were beaten to a pulp.

She missed lining up with such people…such scum.

Ah, they're all lining up to have a go at me. I pulled the plug on her and now I'm plugged into them.

Lester watched the images on the opposite wall with intellectual fascination: The Hindu god of scribes, as one of his duties, creates barriers with his rodent friend, making the maze wandering harder or easier as it suits the seeker of enlightenment.

He turned to the narrow book cabinet for inspiration, if not salvation. His eyes flicked on Carol's copy of *The Decameron*, which they'd read aloud together on hot summer nights before they bought air conditioning.

He felt a pang of jealousy, unbidden but deep. Was this all a ruse to cheat on him with some unknown lover?

Oh God, he covered his eyes: the horrible things literature does.

How can I…

He looked at the bookshelf again, got up, and pulled a Samuel Clemens' collection of Tom Sawyer's adventures off the shelf, cracked it open and read:

"…There's lots of such things, and *they* educate a person…; but there's forty *million* lots of the other kind- the kind that don't happen the same way twice- and they ain't no real use, they ain't more instructive than the small pox. When you've got it, it ain't no good to get vaccinated afterwards, because the small pox don't come but once. But…the person that took a bull by the tail once learnt sixty or seventy times as much as the person that hadn't…"

How many children did Twain have to bury? Lester wasn't certain, and didn't feel like checking his encyclopedia.

The apocalypse can arrive when it wants to, but I don't want to be caught crying or stuck in a book's commercial for living.

Lester sat cross-legged on the floor. He closed the book and thought about his trip to South Dakota the previous summer to see the Black Hills, the Badlands, and Mount Rushmore. Perhaps the little creatures dancing around the room, emerging from the walls, floor, and ceiling were just souvenirs from the Indians. Instead of snapshots, visions. Maybe someday we'll have children- NO!- and I can tell them tall tales based on my sojourn to Paha Sapa and the aftermath.

Feeling better, Lester turned on a cable TV news channel and heard through the quilt that American forces were dropping supplies of food as well as bombs on the Afghani people. Buddhists were cheering on the attack against the Taliban who had desecrated or destroyed several ancient Buddhist monuments.

Recalling his Shiva stories, Lester wondered if he is to be the demon who decapitates Ganesha and finds an elephant-head as a replacement. He remembered the movie Carol had brought home from the library: an old black and white flick with towering plaster elephant statues to symbolize the greatness of Babylon, now rotting somewhere in a Hollywood wasteland.

Oh no, he thought: Even Carol is in on it. A vast conspiracy played out: I have the duty of taking Ganesha's head without all the benefits of being Shiva! And what do I get? Visions of animals!

Tell me *No Wire Hangers!* as a Broadway musical is part of my hallucination. I don't think I could bear a rich movie mommy beating her adopted daughter with a coat-hanger being churned out as fodder from New York City to us hicks in the Midwest. I'd rather stay with Shiva; at least he reshaped Ganesha with a duty in mind. Broadway is running on fumes with versions of cartoons and old movies revamped for the stage.

Reformed, Lester laughed: Reformed to idealize the cosmic prank.

6.

The Optics of Metaphysics

Barbara walked into the Saint John's art studio as Webley finished cleaning his brushes. She said hello and he replied, "Hi Babsy, how ya doing?"

"I'm fine."

"Good. Glad to hear it."

She turned on the radio, dabbed with paint, and switched it to her favorite station.

"Aagh," Webley said. "Am I the only one at this school who can work without a constant noise?"

"You're leaving, aren't you?"

"As a matter of fact, I am."

Barbara got out her painting from where it was stored in its niche and set up her easel, saying, "Well, then it won't disturb you."

"It already has: it's ruined my satori."

"If a little noise can ruin your satori then you must not be very enlightened."

Webley laughed, "Impeccable logic, Babsy dear. I know, maybe a rock and roll version of the *Bible* will lead me to the state of all bliss."

"You're such a snob, Webley."

"Better still, a Broadway musical that was a movie first forty years ago. That'll really make me an art snob. Hanging out with you hicks in Iowa has given me a deep appreciation for the high art of New York City. In fact, I think I'll go down to the slaughterhouse and buy an eviscerated cow, varnish it, and use it as part of my final show. But I don't know if the teachers would understand the subtle nuances of it. However, if I could get an advertising agency to give me a million and a half bucks for it, then I'm certain most critics would appreciate it and hail me as the genius that I am for creating a contemporary golden calf."

Barbara set up her paints as Webley- probably high, Barbara thought- rattled on, "It truly is ironic that if one is critical of art then one simply doesn't "get" it. To boil down thousands of years of art criticism into such a simple phrase has me wonder that civilization is still around. Did you know the Philistines were more advanced than the Jews? It's true. Yet due to the subjectivity of history, the Philistines became associated with barbarism. A modern parallel would be someone rewriting Shakespeare's *The Tempest* into a TV show about a hurricane that shipwrecks seven people on an island and their adventures. Well, so long, Babs. I'll leave on this note."

He flicked off the lights and went out the door.

The sun was still bright and the shades were up so Barbara had no trouble finding the switch. As she began to paint, she heard Webley's voice calling her from outside. She went to a half open window and leaned out. Webley asked if she was going out that night and she replied probably.

"I'll meet you at Lunar's, okay?"

"Okay, Webley. I hope you feel better having gotten all that out of your system."

Barbara painted for two and a half hours until it began getting dark. She put her painting in a corner to dry and cleaned up quickly, wondering at how fast time had gone by. Perhaps, she thought, it'd be better to work at home, where the only sounds were Joyce going about her activities and the guy upstairs playing records on his turntable. Barbara clicked off the lights and radio and walked to the lower level, where she picked up a copy of the school newspaper from a stack near the exit doors.

She made her way home, smelling lilacs and passing under a blossoming tree that blew white petals on her from a gentle breeze. Just like in the movies, she thought. A car slowed down as it passed her and she thought of using Joyce's advice of holding her hand to her head and talking aloud as if she were using a cell-phone. Joyce could pull something like that off, Barbara thought: I don't have the guts for it. She sighed audibly when the car sped off.

She noticed the streetlights were on and stepped up her pace. She unlocked the front door and waved to Joyce, who was sitting on the sofa in the living room, talking on the phone, saying, "Oh, Barbara just came in."

Barbara went to the kitchen where the bass thumping from upstairs kept an arrhythmic beat. She got out the makings for a cheese and hot pepper omelet. A few moments later, Joyce walked in and sat at the kitchen table.

"That was my brother."

"Oh? How's he doing?"

"Pretty good. He had the funniest story. Oh, you're making an omelet? Can you make it real big and I'll share?"

"I suppose so. But you'll owe me a few eggs."

"Okay. Anyway, he was at the bus stop for school, you know, waiting with little Tammy, when one of her classmates showed up chewing a big wad of gum and counting out his Goofy Gaffe stickers."

"What's that?" Barbara asked.

"Oh, the same kind of some collectible junk that every generation has. The guy upstairs probably owns them all. So this kid is tearing open packages, trying to find the rare one to complete his collection and his brother says, 'Where'd you get the money for those?' And the other kid said, 'I found it.' His brother says, 'No you didn't. Mom had $20 in her purse and you took it.' 'No I didn't.' 'I'm gonna tell mom.' And his brother took off and ten minutes later a car pulls up and his mom gets out and starts kicking the boy in the ass all the way to the car. 'Ma, ma, I didn't do it!' 'Yes you did. Get in there and quit lying.' The kid was dropping his stickers and said, 'But ma, my stickers!' 'I don't give a shit! Get in the car.' About halfway through first period the kid showed up at school with a little bruise on his cheek. Tammy asked him if his mom hit him and he says no, he fell down some steps."

"Joyce, how can you laugh at that?"

"Don't you think it's funny? My brother said they're not a very well off family and the kid probably spent all their grocery money on that trash. Though who knows? Maybe in twenty or thirty years they'll be worth a couple hundred thousand bucks."

Barbara shook her head, "I don't see how you can be a professional in that area and laugh about it."

"It's so funny the way people handle things differently. If she was sent to me for child abuse, I wouldn't make a big deal out of one incident like that. The kid's in fourth grade; he should know better. Remember the Mexicans at the shopping center?"

Barbara and Joyce had gone to a local grocery store and while Barbara did the shopping, Joyce had inconspicuously followed a family of Hispanics. Two boys, in their preteens, got some canned muck to play with and their little sister, about four-years-old, couldn't bear it. She sobbed and threw herself on the floor again and again while her mother patiently picked her up and tried to calm her. Finally, the mother handed the little girl a kaleidoscope and the tears immediately stopped.

"That girl was such a ham," Joyce said. "I've never seen anyone throw a fake tantrum like her. My mom wouldn't fall for that."

"But would've she hit you?"

"No. She just would've outlasted me."

Joyce set places at the table while Barbara cooked the omelet. Barbara asked, "Do you have plans tonight?"

"Not really. The tracksters invited me to Demosberg, but their designated driver always gets drunk. I don't want to end up on the ten o'clock news as a cautionary story about drinking and driving. I did feel like dancing with a black guy, though. There're some in Demosberg who aren't too scurvy."

"We could go to Lunar's Pub."

"I thought you didn't like it."

"Well, Webley said he was going."

"Oh, no. The man who would be Michelangelo but usually settles for existential angst."

*** *** ***

Webley was sitting alone in a booth when Joyce and Barbara arrived at the club. Joyce excused herself, saying she was going to the second level where there was a dance floor. Barbara ordered a diet beer and joined Webley, sitting across from him. They made small talk for a few minutes, then Webley asked if she was ready for her final show.

"Just about," she said. "All I need is approval for my last painting."

"Yeah. Beerstocky really screwed us around on that, didn't he?"

Cal Bertsowski had graduated the previous year. At his final show, he unveiled a beautifully done painting of graphic sex scenes starring himself and several of the most attractive women on campus, including a professor of economics. The powers-that-be were not amused and a strict ordinance that commanded the instructors' approval for final show was instituted.

"Yeah," Barbara said, "it only takes one person to ruin things for everyone else."

"You gotta admit though, it was a great painting."

"Of course it was, from a male's point of view."

"Oh, come on. It was the best painting last year."

"I preferred Marilyn's show."

"Right. I bet you can't describe any one of her paintings."

Barbara puzzled for a moment and said, "You're right. They were great scenic paintings but I can't remember any of them in particular. Still, she was better than Clarence."

Webley laughed, "Oh, come on. Finding inspiration from rock and roll album sleeves is high art."

"I heard he's working for an advertising agency."

"Fitting. Say, have you bought any pot recently?"

"No," Barbara shook her head. "I don't have time for it. How about you?"

"Well, I bought some, man, but I don't know. Did you get any news from grad schools?"

"The U of Iowa turned me down."

"Count your blessings."

"Well, I might try them again." She furrowed her brow. "You've got a real chip on your shoulder about Iowa City."

"For good reason," Webley said. "Haven't you seen the art they have decorating the riverbank?"

"I don't remember it. Joyce was in a hurry to get to her sister's."

"It's just a bunch of twisted metal. At first I thought they were furnace pipes, you know, leading from the art building; but no, it's somebody's sculpture."

"Well, what do you expect? I mean, they want something outside that can withstand the elements."

"So why not a totem pole?"

"Because," Barbara replied, "some drunken frat rats would probably demolish it."

"See? That's exactly what I mean. If it was great art someone would ruin it, so the sophisticos have to cater to the lowest common denominator."

"Why do you take things like that so personally?"

Webley said, "Because they want my approval, and if I don't give it to them then I'm inartistic and close-minded."

"I don't think they really care about your opinion, Webley."

"Well, they sure care about their own."

Barbara sighed inwardly and asked, "Will you be ready in time for your final show?"

"I'm not sure. I hope so. I've been doing a lot of reading and getting some good ideas."

"Oh? Like what?"

"I got through Milton's *Paradise Regained* after about three months. It's incredibly visionary, almost hallucinatory."

"Really?"

"Yeah. I'm sort of planning a painting based on Christ's temptations in the desert. In one part I'll show Lucifer's visions to Jesus, and his refusal to partake of them. Then I'll paint

Christ offering the same sorts of things to the hallucinating Saint John, only at the apex, instead of being crowned with the kingdoms of the world, I'll have a crucifix."

"Wow. That sounds good. I hope you get to paint it. Maybe if you lay off the pot…"

"Yeah," Webley said, "I know. I'll go get us a pitcher."

"Be sure to get my flavor or you'll have to drink the whole thing yourself."

"Wouldn't that be a pity?"

Barbara sat watching people come and go. After ten minutes, she turned to look for Webley. He was standing at the far end of the bar talking to one of his bong-buddies. For a moment, she flashed hatred; then she took a small notebook and pen out of her purse and began sketching a self-portrait.

Several long moments later, Webley returned with a pitcher of beer. "I'm sorry," he said. "I had to take care of some business."

"Buying more pot?"

He shook his head. "Dithers brought in a bunch of weed and everyone he's sold it to is hallucinating. I'm trying to find out what it was sprayed with."

"You're tripping?"

"Yeah, and it's not very pleasant. The good news is the Flubbies won again."

"Oh my, that is good news."

"A little less sarcasm, please. Tonight I need all the victories I can get."

"Well, we've covered religion and art. What next? Politics?"

"Oh no," he said. "No, there might be some interesting conspiracy theories about Marseilles burning to the ground for no apparent reason, but I'm not going to get into a debate about the war with Iraq."

"Why not? You're one of the few people I know who is really pro-war."

"You'd really fit in with Iowa City: they love protesting everything."

"And you don't?"

"I'm more realistic than you. I don't fall for the liberal versus conservative stuff."

"Right," Barbara laughed. "You're so realistic that you're stoned out of your mind."

Webley made a face, then laughed with her. "Okay, okay. I deserved that. But, you know, here's a little known fact for you. Ronald Reagan was portrayed as this staunch white racist conservative and Bill Clinton, though I should say Baal because he's more like an out-of-control sex demon; anyway, he was imaged as this soft-hearted liberal. But actually, the prison rate, especially among black males, went up more under Clinton than Reagan."

"I didn't know that."

"Not many people do. It was the ripple effect of the "three crimes and you're in prison" policy."

"But doesn't Bush Junior's Bible-banging disturb you?"

"It could be worse. At least he's not pounding the *Koran* or the *Old Testament.* You're better off as a non-believer in his crusades than you would be if you were a dissident in Israel or a Muslim country. Besides, in a couple years, with any luck, he'll be voted out."

"I don't think he'll let that happen."

"Neither do I," Webley shrugged. "Especially since the Democrats give him just about everything he wants...then, at election time, tell us how different they are from him."

Joyce showed up with a young black man she introduced as Clemente. Webley asked, "Are you named after the baseball player?"

"Give that man a cigar," Clemente said.

After a few moments, Clemente and Joyce returned upstairs because she heard a song to which she wanted to dance.

Webley said, "Seems like a nice enough guy. He must have driven in from Demosberg."

"Where did you get your name from?"

"Oh, some book my parents read. You know Aldous Huxley?"

"I read *Brave New World.*"

"You should read *The Doors of Perception,*" Webley said. "I'll loan you my copy."

"That's where they got the name?"

"Huh? Oh. No. They got it from another novel of his that I haven't read. I think it was *Point Counter-Point.* One of the interesting things he wrote about was how we all try to live out our favorite fictional characters. For instance, you'd like to be one of the heroines from a Jane Austen novel."

"Yeah, and you'd like to be Lucifer from *Paradise Regained.*"

"Oh, come on now," Webley said. "I haven't tempted you with any grass."

"You just haven't gotten around to it yet."

Webley put his hands over his eyes and sobbed, "Maybe I should be a blind bard."

"I'm just kidding, Webley," she said, touching his arm. "Really."

Several moments later he pulled his hands from his face, smiling.

"That's not cool," Barbara said. "I mean, I thought you were on a bummer trip."

"I was. But then I started thinking about the humor of being Lucifer and tripping with Jesus. When you think about it, Christ really learned a lot from the experience."

"Like what?"

"How to tempt people with illusions. It's our inheritance of art: to craft fantasies to convince people that beliefs in illusions are better than the reality of this dimension. For instance, there is no such thing as color; like Newton proved, color is only a conglomeration of atoms and molecules reflecting light. While I'm hallucinating, I'm not just seeing things that aren't there, but rather molecules and atoms of things that form future and past events. Of course, I wouldn't say that to a psychologist because they'd just dope me up on some brand of pharmaceutical medication."

"You'd end up on 2-west."

"The psycho ward," Webley nodded.

"How come you never went to visit Phil while he was there? He asked about you."

"Oh, those places make me nervous. Besides, I think I preferred him as a prophet than someone in hospital jammies and slippers. Do you want to get out of here and get some pizza?"

"In a little while. I'm having a good time. Aren't you?"

"Yeah," Webley said. "It just seems too crowded."

"You know, I forgot about there being no such thing as color. It's an interesting thing to hear from a painter."

"Kind of nihilistic, isn't it?"

"Very," Barbara said. "It makes my head spin."

"I read somewhere that Newton was into alchemy."

"Like gold from lead?"

"That's part of it," Webley shook his head. "I don't understand most of it. Or want to, for that matter. But it'd be an interesting subject for a painting: a black sun, androgynous twins. That kind of stuff. I've wondered how to go about painting the fact that there is no color."

"That's too heady for me. I'll stick to portraits."

"At least you've found what you're good at."

"Yeah," Barbara said, "but it's outdated. Even rich people aren't interested in having their portraits done. It's so much easier to be photographed."

"What about Saddam Hussein?"

"Right. And have all my paintings torn down."

"Well, there're plenty of oil-rich sheiks in other countries who'd appreciate your talents."

"I don't want to convert to Islam."

"Tempting, though," Webley said, "isn't it?"

"Not really. I imagine most of the painters in those countries are men."

"Probably. It wouldn't be very easy to paint with a veil over your face."

Barbara nodded, "I could go to California and do portraits of the New Age gods and goddesses for the cults."

"I bet you could do a real good Buddha. And they probably wouldn't be strict about you believing in all that nonsense."

"You think Buddhism is nonsense?"

"No, I think their trendy interpretations of it is nonsense. Did you see where some nuns' convent had a painting contest and the winner was a portrait of a black Jesus surrounded by things like the yin and yang symbols and other non-Christian signs?"

"No," Barbara said, "I must have missed that."

"Well, there you go. Do a portrait of the Virgin Mother and smear it with elephant-dung and you're a sure winner. You could call it Mudonher."

"I doubt I have the nerve to do that."

"You ready to go?"

"Let's see what Joyce is doing."

"Ah, I'm getting out of here. You coming?"

"No, I'm not hungry."

Webley left the booth muttering, "Bitch."

Barbara sat bolt upright for a moment, then yelled, "Asshole!" She turned to look at him, saw he was smiling and she gritted her teeth. She ignored the people looking at her questioningly and went upstairs. She found Joyce and pulled her into the ladies' room.

"What's wrong?" Joyce asked over the pounding music.

"Webley. We were getting along so well and then he called me a bitch."

"Oh god. You two. Well, come join us. We're having a good time."

"No. I want to go home."

"Why? Don't let him spoil the night."

"Please, Joyce. Let's just go home."

"Well, I'll have one of the guys give you a ride."

"No," Barbara said, "they're all drunk."

"Could you call a cab?"

"I don't want to get in the habit of using taxis. It's too expensive."

"Well, then, you're going to have to hit your parents up for a cell-phone because I'm getting tired of this. You should know better than to hang out with Webley. Especially after what he did."

"Will you come then?"

"Yeah. But you owe me for this. Big time. Give me a minute to tell them I'm leaving."

The next morning, Barbara walked to the studio. As she passed a group of young men who were going in the opposite direction, she recognized them as the crew Joyce was with the previous night. They gave each other hellos and as they moved on, she heard one say in a falsetto voice, "Oh, please don't touch me! I've been raped!"

There was laughter and one of them said, "Don't say that, man. What if she was your sister?"

She told them, Barbara thought: She told them.

Fifteen minutes later three patrol cars pulled up in front of Joyce and Barbara's apartment. The police went inside and pulled Barbara off a bleeding mound of unconscious human flesh.

7.

The Democratic Theory of Evolution

Sam Nead stopped by the tavern for a beer and a tenderloin sandwich to go. He was mostly ignored by the other patrons, however Buzz Cauldron said, "Been meaning to ask where you're from."

"New York City," Sam answered.

"Is that where your tribe is?"

"No."

"You left the safety of the reservation to get bombed in New York?"

"Who said I got bombed?"

"Well, hell, boy, you lead such a cloistered life you never heard of 911?"

"Yeah," Sam said, "that's an emergency number. I think it's the name of a TV show too."

"Buzz," said one of his cronies, "you mean 9-11; and the Towers didn't get bombed- well, actually, they did back in '93- but you probably mean the air attacks."

"Well, he knows what I mean."

Sam sat quietly, waiting for his sandwich.

Buzz mulled a few moments, then said, "I know if I got money from the government to live somewhere, I'd take advantage of it."

"And leave your tar-paper shack, Buzz?" another crony said. "I find that hard to believe."

"You mean," Sam asked, "they give money out just for being Indian?"

"But ya gotta live on your reservation," Buzz affirmed.

"Do you get more money for being full-blood and less if you're a breed?"

"I don't know," Buzz admitted. "I imagine it's the same for everyone."

"Buzz, they get house upkeep money," the first crony said. "Which is probably just enough for a weekend binge at one of their casinos. Kind of like you, with your subsidy farming checks until you got mortgaged out."

Buzz said, "You ought to read this pamphlet I picked up in Demosberg. It'll enlighten you on a few points about the corruption of the government." He passed around the paper, encouraging readers.

"Buzz," an old-timer said, looking at the back of the pamphlet, "did you read who printed this?"

"Well, no. What difference does it make?"

"It's from the Ku Klux Klan for crying out loud."

"So?"

"Buzz, I know it's been a while since you've been to Mass, but they happen to be anti-Papacy."

"Huh?"

"They hate Catholics almost as much as they hate niggers and Jews."

Buzz sat frowning and a crony said, "Now leave the deacon alone and quit bringing this kind of trash around. Next thing you know you'll be sporting a swastika on your forehead and we'll have to kick your ass just like we done to the Nazis."

As Sam paid for his meal, one of the older men said, "When I was in the Navy during World War II we caught two faggots getting it on under a bunk-bed. My buddy whacked one over the head with a flashlight and busted it so that the batteries went flying everywhere. I told him, 'Hold on there! Don't kill him.'"

Sam drove the three blocks to his small house, wondering if he should trade in his foreign made car for an American pick-up truck. He chose to wait until after his meeting with Father Sangle before making a decision.

He put some condiments on the tenderloin and got out a bag of potato chips. He drank a glass of fruit punch and ate while watching the local news. How different, he thought, than the news in New York City. In the lead story, a farmer showed off a litter of albino pigs; then there was a long segment on a teenage party two nights previous, which had been busted by local cops and the state highway patrol. Sam muttered aloud, "I guess it's ridiculous to expect any news on the Pope being wracked-up by Parkinson's Disease." During beer commercials, Sam flicked the channel to cartoons.

Bugs Bunny and Yosemite Sam were running for an elected office. Bugs did a Teddy Roosevelt imitation, saying he talked softly and carried a big stick. Yosemite Sam responded, 'I talk loudly and carry a bigger stick! And I use it too!' Whereupon he took a swing at Bugs's head.

Sam watched, thinking it more entertaining than the Democratic Presidential nominees worming out of the woodwork for the 2004 elections. Indeed, when Al Gore made his losing bid in 2000 he spent much of his campaign saying he would do everything George Bush Junior would do, only bigger and better. Which, at the time, was a curious thing, particularly concerning the increase in military spending; for, except for the Pentagon and the armament manufacturers with their consistent crying for money, there was no general call to increase military spending. Now, three years later, it was truly amazing to watch Americans spend trillions of dollars while cutting taxes. It was evident that the media embraced extensive presidential campaigns due to the money received for candidates' ads, and not having to cover real news, except what a wannabe spent on a haircut.

Well, Sam thought, Bush Junior said he wanted to be like Ronald Reagan and deficit spending sure is one way to mimic him. The thing about Bush Junior is he's unafraid to parody himself: he was proud to be photographed holding a copy of a humor magazine, just so the publishers would put him on the cover. He brags about his mediocre grades to graduating classes. When did all the dignity go out of the office? Now everyone, including the President, wants to be first with a punch line.

However, except for seeing him dress up like a soldier, something Caligula was noted for, he hadn't recently been a public embarrassment, Sam thought. Since the air attacks, Bush Junior doesn't seem quite as smarmy. He still smirks like a 10-year-old who's just pulled a prank, however he does seem more refined.

Sam took off his jeans and t-shirt and put on a pair of dress slacks and a button-down shirt. He had another hour before meeting Father Sangle so Sam sat at his desk to look over the papers for his 12th grade religion class. He found the smartest pupil's essay and read an exegesis on Samuel, the kingmaker of early Israel.

The thesis was complex: Saul was not permitted to wheel-and-deal with non-Jewish tribes, unlike David, because Saul was not as advanced in bartering for power for the Chosen People. David learned from Saul's mistakes to have truces with outside tribes, which could be broken at the slightest instigation, or play the pagan tribes off of one another in wars. Part of Samuel's realization from Yaweh was that bartering with outsiders was only to be done if they could not be wiped-out in bloody sprees called Bans. The student wrote a parallel to the 1980's deals between America, Iraq, and Afghanistan: the rulers of the latter countries were useful in fighting American enemies like Iran and the U.S.S.R.; then George Bush Junior, a born again Christian, took it as his duty to God and America to destroy Iraq's Saddam Hussein and Afghanistan's Taliban, who had apparently outlived their usefulness. John Ashcroft, who couldn't win a Congressional race against a dead man, was installed as the supreme law leader: another born again Christian, seeming to fancy himself a judge like the pre-king era of Israel.

Sam marked the paper A+ and drove to Sacred Heart Church. He still had fifteen minutes until the meeting, so he sat in a pew, enjoying the cool darkness. He watched the votive candles flickering from the offerings on each side of the altar and remembered the cave in Yosemite Park where Marion and he were followed by a family of tourists.

"I hope the lights don't go out and we can't find our way back," the father of the family said. "I don't want to get lost in here with Injun Joe."

"Me eat um your young," Sam grunted. "Take um your wife."

The laughter from the family had pleased Sam, however, when they got outside, Marion sternly refused their invitation to join them for an ice cream.

"What's wrong?" Sam asked as they walked to his motorcycle.

"I didn't find his racist comments- and you going along with it- very funny."

"It was just a dumb joke. What was I supposed to do? Stand there and lecture him on the plight of Native Americans?"

"There's lots of things you could've done instead of having them laugh at some stereotypical Indian joke."

"Not everyone is enlightened, Marion. We all have portions of ourselves locked away in caverns where they flit around like albino bats."

Ah, Sam thought, another lost love affair.

He checked his watch and went to a side-door, which led to a sidewalk that branched one way towards the parking lot and the other to the priests' quarters. He knocked on Father Sangle's door and was answered with a "Come in."

The old man had his air conditioning on and was sitting in his living room recliner. "Sam, my boy, you look good."

"Thank you. Where do you want me to sit?"

"Well, I thought we could go into the conference room. Here, follow me." The priest stood up slowly, carrying a file.

They walked down a darkened hallway, Sam wondering at the unexpected formality of the occasion. Father Sangle had queer ideas about privacy. On more than one occasion he'd met Sam at the door in pajamas and a robe and taken him into the conference room as if it were the priest's apartment. Now, however, he was in his clerical black, complete with white collar.

They sat at opposite sides of the table and the priest asked, "How have you been doing?"

"Oh fine. Just fine."

"That's good. This hot weather hasn't been getting you down?"

"No," Sam shook his head; "it doesn't bother me a bit."

"Good. Well, the reason I called you in is to go over the test scores with you." Father Sangle opened the file and took out a sheet of paper. "There seem to be some anomalies in your answers."

"Oh? Like what?"

"Without going into detail, some sexual tendencies."

Sam laughed, startling the priest. "You mean the dog question."

"Well, among others."

"I've never had sex with a dog, Father; however, when I was a kid my family had a German Shepard that used to mount my leg, so of course I did think about having sex with a dog because it was fairly obvious that was what she was after."

"But you didn't desire to have sex with her?"

"No," Sam said. "But that wasn't the question on the test; the question was, have I ever thought about it."

"Well, your frankness is astonishing. I take it you have had thoughts of...having sex with children?"

Sam kept smiling, "I was dating a woman once who had a few kids. One of them said she was going to kiss my pee-pee. I told her that no she wasn't. So the thought was there, though the desire wasn't."

Father Sangle shook his head, "I find your levity quite alarming. We can't possibly accept you as a seminarian with this kind of score. And your cavalier attitude towards it seems to indicate that you don't care."

Sam wiped his mouth, taking the grin from his face. "Oh, I do care, Father. Otherwise I wouldn't be so honest."

"To tell you the truth," the priest said, putting his hand flat on the folder, "this is enough to remove you from your position at Sacred Heart."

Sam sat stunned. After a moment he said, "It's that bad?"

"It makes you seem a menace to children."

"I'd never act on those thoughts, Father. And they don't haunt my every step. They just occur on occasion and I shrug them off and don't think about them any more."

Father Sangle leaned back and blew out a sigh. "You use truth as a weapon, Sam, and I'm afraid this time its turned on you. The Church is in a crisis and you seem to take it as a joke."

"I wouldn't be a pedophile priest, Father. Sometimes, because of the way I was raised, I laugh at horrible things. Even Dante learned to laugh at the torments of hell."

Father Sangle shook his head. "That's not the issue. There are certain things expected from seminarians and one of them is to not take things like this lightly."

"Well maybe if I took it again…"

"You'd give us the answers we want. But that's not the point either. What if ten years from now you get accused of molestation. How would-"

"But I wouldn't-"

"No. Now listen. I didn't say you would do anything. I just said if you were accused. What do you think would happen when they dig through your records and found this? What kind of defense would you or the Church have?"

"I suppose you can't just make that disappear, huh?"

"It would be a disservice to the parish."

"Does that mean I'm fired?"

"I don't have that authority," the priest said. "However, I suspect your contract won't be renewed at the end of the school year."

"I guess that explains why the principal has been avoiding me like the plague."

"I'm sorry it worked out this way, Sam."

Sam bit back on a scathing remark about the pasty skin of the old priest reminding Sam of a leper.

He drove back to his bungalow and checked his bank account book. He had enough savings to leave Stillwater at the end of the semester, though where he would go he was not certain. He sat at his desk and printed A+ on all the papers, even the six copies that were all the same, obviously downloaded off the Internet. Give them what they want, Sam thought: If I flunked them their parents would protest that I was making it more difficult for their cheating babies to get into college.

Sam wrote in his journal: The migrations of Indians to America divided them into city dwellers and nomads. After a few thousand years, the genetic lineages became attuned to their particular lifestyles. A large part of duality is specialization. One of the banes of education is teaching that everyone and their cultural symbols are equal. The *I-Ching* and Dante's *Divine*

Comedy are both cultural high points, yet they are not equal. The semantics of equality means both works are interchangeably the same.

To finish off his evening's work, Sam took out the book of poetry Marion had given him, used a black pen to scratch out "Truth is beauty and beauty is truth" and wrote: Truth is an albino hiding in the recesses of our souls.

8.

Onanism

He pushed the bonelike structure to one side and observed the sac. He touched it gently and it was tender and swollen. He opened the medicine cabinet and took out a razor. He held it under hot water and when the heat became unbearable, he held the steel head of the razor to the sac, using the tool as a catalyst to liquefy a blast of fluid. He winced, then quickly put the razor down, pushed the bonelike structure aside and squeezed the sac as hard as he could, watching with satisfaction the gunk splatter on the mirror. The best one yet: a true gusher. He tentatively touched it and the spot was sore and angry red.

That, he thought, was better than a really snot-filled sneeze. He carelessly wiped the zit-juice off the mirror with toilet paper, checked his nose again to see if the skin had broken and peeled from the pimple, then got ready for school.

He had given up on most clothes, settling for pants with expanding waistlines. For a few years he had bought pants for taller men who matched his weight size; however, he had better ways of spending his money than paying a seamstress to take in the foot-cuffs.

He ejected the cassette from the video player and put it in its box. He briefly wondered about buying a pistol to conceal on his bulk in case some punk at school was inspired by all the news stories of shooting classmates. He sighed, shook his head, and placed *Taxi Driver* in its appropriate alphabetical niche.

He ate the leftover fast-food chicken sandwich as a breakfast dessert and washed it down with a soda. He brushed his teeth, thinking of his last medical examination. His doctor had bluntly told him if he didn't lose weight he would host a variety of physical problems, including diabetes and heart troubles. His doctor suggested a 12-Step food addiction program.

Stillwater had no meetings and he didn't want to make long distance calls to find one, so he settled for Alcoholics Anonymous. He went to one meeting, listened attentively, and swore off the occasional Saturday six-pack. However, he could not find the wherewithal to substitute in the 12-Steps his food craving for alcohol; though he did find himself desiring coffee and a cigarette.

He ate the last long john, laughing about John F. Kennedy speaking in German to an audience in Berlin, "I am a doughnut!" to a rousing cheer of approval. Each president seemed to offer menus to the public as a sort of communion; news stories abounded over a dislike for asparagus, or a preference for jellybeans.

He drove to the school, not wearing his seatbelt, which wouldn't fit around his waist. It was graduation day for the 8th grade and the final day of classes. He had his 3rd grade students make a drawing of the influential things in their lives as part of the open house show for visiting parents. When finished, the students hung them on a bulletin board without signing them to make a challenge for parents to guess which was done by their child. He perused them, startled by a well-crafted drawing of a fat man with an elephant head, surrounded by dishes of food.

He pulled it off the board, not caring if it ripped, crying, "Is this someone's idea of a joke?"

The students sat bolt upright, a few quivering with fear.

"Who did this? Tell me who did this."

After a long silence, an Indian girl sobbed, "It's Ganesha!" and hung her head.

"Who?" He stood over the girl, waiting for her to rat-out the culprit. When she cringed and began to curl up, he gently lifted her chin and asked, "Just tell me who did this."

"It's Ganesha. My god of good luck and humor."

He closed his eyes and turned his head upward. "I'm very sorry. I thought...Well, during math you can do another picture."

He waddled back to his desk and the children returned to their history books. He thought: Maybe I'm only confrontational with the small and weak. It was much different than seeing my ex-wife again.

She had arrived unannounced at his apartment the previous Sunday and her greeting was less than cordial, "But my, you've gotten big!"

Instead of saying, 'What's it to you, ----', he had shrugged, "Hello."

"I didn't mean to disturb you from TV- especially if there's girls' gymnastics on- but I figured you wouldn't be at church or anywhere else."

"Yeah," he said. "And?"

She tried to squeeze by his bulk blocking the door and for a moment he didn't budge; then allowed her into the kitchen. She glanced around, commenting, "I'd forgotten how big the kitchen is. It's a shame you don't use it."

"Yeah, I cry myself to sleep over it every night."

She patted his belly, saying, "Just for luck. Like the Buddha at Mi Loos." They had eaten there on their first date and were told to rub the laughing statue's stomach for good fortune.

He could feel the energy to stand his ground against her slowly drain; as if a large needle had been stuck into his conscious will power, what little he had, and sapped every defense mechanism. He even thought of asking her to sit down and then trying some awkward romance.

"Well," she said, before he could blurt anything, "you can probably guess this isn't a social visit. I'm here to get my uncle's silverware."

He frowned, "I thought you already had it."

"I thought so too, but I've looked everywhere and can't find them."

"Well, I'll look for it and when I have it I'll call."

"I hate to seem pushy," she said, "but I'm cooking a special meal for a male friend tonight and want them now."

"Okay. Go ahead and look. I'm going to watch TV."

After fifteen minutes of searching, she went into the living room, stood in front of the TV and said, "I can't find them. Did you pawn it for some porno phone calls or to support your fast-food diet?" She laughed humorlessly.

He was so surprised by the attack he didn't become wrathful; instead, he shook his head and said, "No."

"Will you help me look?"

"Okay. Go back in the bedroom and I'll see if they're around here."

He went to the small cubbyhole that he called Anne Frank's safe house, moved the hardcore girly magazines aside on the shelf and found the silverware kit.

She snatched it, saying, "You knew where they were all along."

"It just happened to be the first place I checked."

"You're still a fat ferret," she said, slamming the door behind her.

He thought: Wouldn't a packrat be a better metaphor? After all, the only reason he'd stayed in their apartment was he'd collected too much stuff to make a move worthwhile and feasible.

As the students went to the baccalaureate, he glumly followed at a distance, still ashamed of his unprovoked explosion. The principal, a lean, balding man, stepped beside him and asked if he'd care to go to Flubbies tavern after the open house to celebrate in an adult manner. Pleasantly surprised, he said yes. He'd heard from the rumor-mill that the principal waxed philosophical after a few drinks, and perhaps he could be enlightening on a few matters. It was the first time he had been invited anywhere by a colleague since his divorce.

He had a greasy Reuben sandwich while waiting for the principal at Flubbies. He arrived twenty minutes later and waved him to a secluded table. He nursed a beer while the principal ordered gin and tonic, which he drained half of with his first drink; then he said, "I heard you had a bit of a meltdown in class today."

"One of the students tell you?"

"Nah," the principal said. "The recess monitor found that Indian girl cowering in a corner of the playground. Apparently, you terrified the ---- out of her."

"It was just a misunderstanding."

"Don't worry," the principal said; "I really didn't care to hear the sob story. Having a large girth used to be a sign of wealth and prosperity. Now it's just another symbol of how ----ed up America is. Personally, I'm getting tired of coddling new generations."

"Then you chose a contrary business."

The principal shrugged, "I used to be able to kick them around a bit to keep them in line. Now I can't even get my morning paper without some neighborhood punk calling me a bald, grouchy old ----. As far as I'm concerned they should re-institute the military draft for every 18-year-old, male and female. Get the little buggers to toe-the-line."

"They may have to do it anyway to support the wars."

"Things won't go well in Iraq unless we cut off the oil war profiteers and bring in the United Nations bloc to manage the war and do their own profiteering."

"I doubt Halliburton would allow that."

"What'll probably happen," the principal said, "is American companies will run Iraq's oil industry and our troops will be the corporations' guards. Then we'll wonder why the Iraqis are pissed off at us as the oil companies steal their main resource and sell it to China."

"You don't think it'll come here?"

"Nah. The oil companies can make more money selling it to other countries, starting a shortage here so the prices will go up."

"It's curious that Americans associate freedom with convenience and transient objects. When I was a boy I learned in school that our needs are air, food, and water; everything else is a want."

The principal laughed, "During my war with my ex-wife we battled over who would get the large screen TV, and in court I found out TV is no longer considered a luxury item but a necessity."

"So who won?"

"Ah, I let the ---- have it because I moved in with a woman who already had one."

"Did you get remarried?"

"Yeah. That's why I don't take communion."

"Oh, that's right: automatic excommunication."

The principal nodded, "And that old hard-on priest would've made a show of not giving it to me. Fortunately, I'm close enough to retirement that I'm not affected by the school not renewing my contract."

"I hadn't heard that."

"Ah, the ----heads waited until after graduation to announce it."

"Does it bother you that you can't take the sacraments any more?"

The principal said, "The Church is so ----ed up that it doesn't matter to me. Kennedy bought an annulment so he could marry again in the Church. To paraphrase a parable, when God planted my seed, he must've put it in a stony patch of weeds, so it really isn't my fault."

"It's strange how Boccaccio, Chaucer, and Rabelais wrote humorous stories of how the Catholic clergy were driven by lust. Now all the stories are about sickos."

"It won't be long before a pedophile does the ceremony for queer weddings."

"I've always thought if heterosexuals took marriage more seriously then queers wouldn't be able to make it an issue."

"You're divorced, aren't you?" the principal asked.

"Yeah."

"Ever thought of getting remarried?"

"Oh sure," he said, scratching his head. "But I'm not attracted to fat women and who in their right mind would want an obese ass like me?"

"There's a sub-culture called chubby chasers; maybe you could go on the computer and find some."

"I don't want a co-dependent."

"Not even if she's a good cook?" the principal asked.

"I live off junk-food. Going back to what you were saying about God's seeds: I remember in college I learned an Egyptian god started the universe by masturbating."

The principal laughed, "So the Big Bang was an act of narcissism? Well, at least it was sex with someone he loved."

"And we're the seeds that floated through space to land among weeds and rocks."

"At least we didn't land in a nuclear radiation dump. It's only a matter of time before mutants evolve." The principal frowned a moment, then said, "I've always kind of fancied reincarnation. Maybe with the destruction of the predators' habitats more of them are being reincarnated as ----ing monsters."

"I never thought of that. Some of them can maybe adjust to being human but others want revenge."

The principal nodded, "And their predator instinct precludes them from ----ing knowing that the revenge machine will doom them as well. Not to sound like a Freudian shrink, but it seems Georgie Junior's Oedipal Complex has sucked America into a revenge play on a global scale; and there's ---- all we can do about it."

"I've heard there's no such thing as victims, only volunteers."

"Sounds like something the Marquis de Sade would say," the principal commented.

"Well, I'm not a sadist, but I read one of his books last year and the basic tenet was if people choose to be Christ-like and suffer woes, there's sure to be folks who use the meek as their whipping-boards for torture, sex, war, etcetera."

"Perhaps," the principal said, "that's why Mohammed wrote a holy book that has justifiable reasons for going to war."

"The Catholic Church is more worried about a man spilling his seed on the ground than trying to follow Christ's lessons to not engage in fights."

"Do you think fighting is a waste of energy?"

"Oh, I can understand battling for clean water and food, but there's a point in fighting for living room that people like Hitler are able to blur in lumpum minds."

The principal nodded, "Not only do we try and plant the seeds of Americanism, we're at the point of killing anyone who wants a different crop."

"Unless it's poppies from Afghanistan to fund covert agencies and keep people here stoned."

"It's curious to watch disenfranchised Americans belly-ache about our uncaring government selling us out, yet ironically most people still ----ing believe in franchising democracy and capitalism."

"That's because we associate it with love. People like to think we only wheel-and-deal with fellow believers."

The principal laughed, "The big thing now is Hate Crimes. Our whole ----ing nation is singling out people we blame for the 9-11 air attacks and we charged into Iraq on a fool's whim. Thousands of people are dying and we don't even know who we're fighting- we just call them the Bad Guys- and yet a crime motivated by hate still gets more media coverage than a wedding in Afghanistan being bombed to the stone-age by U.S. troops. It's okay to kill them but not call them towel-heads."

"When the Air Force dropped the Meals Ready to Eat on the Afghanis in the wilderness it was like angels dropping manna from heaven."

The principal snorted, "Planting our seeds of love."

The discussion abruptly changed to gossip about the school's faculty members and he excused himself twenty minutes later. He drove to a shoe store, bought some sneakers, changed clothes in his apartment, and drove to the high school track. He began trudging around the oval, glad to be alone in his attempt at running.

9.

Millennium

It must have been the summer before I started high school when I met Esther Miriam. My crew and me were at the public swimming pool, taking turns with Snot's goggles to check out the chicks diving off the board. I got tired of lurking around the deep-end, waiting for my turn or a bloody fistfight to break out whenever the chesty blonde in a bikini went off the high-board, so I lied down on my soggy towel.

After a few moments I heard a voice asking, "Giving up already, Huck Finn?"

I sat up and saw a young woman standing over me, a long towel about her torso and another wrapped like a turban around her head. "Did you say something?"

"I asked if you were giving up already. I made a bet on you, you know."

"For what?"

"That you'd end up with the goggles the next time Rebecca went off the board."

"You mean the blonde-"

"Dyed."

"With the big…"

She held her hands in front of her petite bosom and said, "Yes, her."

"Well, Snot's being a jerk about his goggles so I quit." I thought a moment and said, "You're watching us?"

"She's putting on quite a peep-show, isn't she? You know, she's actually a good diver- on the swim team and all that- but she seems to enjoy giving you guys a thrill."

"It's better than playing Shark," I admitted.

Shark was a game we made up when we were about seven. Earlier that summer we'd been diving for loose change to share an ice cream when some of the high school guys muscled in on our territory. We played a listless game of Shark, and Snot kept saying he had to go to the bathroom. He was the kind of guy who would walk out of the best part of a movie to use the toilet, but hold it in while playing a stupid kids' game. Anyway, one of the high school guys dove for something at the bottom of the pool, came up with his treasure, and yelled, "Shit!" The pool was cleared and cleaned and as we got ready to leave one of the lifeguards asked if we'd seen anything. We told him no.

I kicked my friends' towels and gear away to clear a spot and invited her to sit down. She demurred, saying, "I can only stay a minute. We're getting ready to leave."

I looked over at her group of friends and they waved cheerfully. I asked, "What's your name?"

"I," she announced, "am Esther Miriam. And you?"

"Jose. Tell me, how come I've never seen you here before?"

"Oh, we usually go to the Aaron and Moses Country Club." When I looked confused, she laughed, "That's a joke, son, don't you get it?"

I shook my head, "Not really."

"It's the Jewish country club."

"Oh? So today you're slumming, huh?"

"The water at the club is infected with some kind of virus."

"Are you sure Snot wasn't there?" I asked.

"What do you mean? Oh, the guy with mucus dribbling off his chin. Gross. And the water here is already disgusting enough."

"You want to come to my house and make fun of my room?"

"Oh, I didn't mean it like that," she said. "I can tell you're kind of different. Anyway, we didn't feel like swimming at Rebecca's place because she's got the most annoying brothers and sisters. So do you do this all the time?"

"Do what?"

"Degrade women and yourself for cheap thrills?"

"Oh no. Am I going to get the same lecture I got from my mom when she found a girly magazine under my bed?"

"Sounds like she's on the ball."

I shook my head, "She's into all that New Age Feminism stuff. Besides, you say your friend knew what we were doing."

"Good point."

"Say, why don't you give me your phone number? Maybe we could go out some time."

"It doesn't sound like you're Jewish."

"So?"

"Well, I'm not allowed to date yet and when I am, it'll have to be Jewish boys my parents approve of."

"We could lie."

"Oh no," she smiled. "No, as my friends like to tell me, I'm refreshingly honest." There was a pause as we thought this over. "What religion are you?"

I shook my head. "I don't have one. I used to think I was Catholic, like Snot. But he said since I haven't been baptized and uh some other thing, that I'm not."

"That's too bad," she said with real sincerity.

I shrugged, "You get used to it."

"Really? I don't think I could."

I found myself getting nettled and felt like going into the anti-religious' spiel that I'd heard so often from my parents and their friends. Instead I said, "Well, I'm not worried about getting into heaven by being part of the right clique."

"Oh, but it's so much more than that. There're communities, families, and education."

"The right cliques," I repeated, pulling my knees to my chest and wrapping my arms around them. The sun had gone behind a large bank of clouds.

"Well, you have your friends."

I didn't reply what I was thinking: Not for long. Snot was already being considered too uncool to hang out with; if he didn't own goggles, we probably would have shunned him. There was also the chemical factor: the guys who wanted to drink and smoke dope all the time would soon be with other crowds. Plus, the matter of sex.

"I suppose I do," I said, then added: "Well, you're blocking the sun so if you don't want to sit down…"

"Oh. Okay. Goodbye."

"Goodbye," I said, lying back down, trying to keep myself from shivering due to the chills. "Tell God hi for me. And next time wear a two-piece-suit and I'll be looking for you."

*** *** ***

I think it was two summers later when we met again because we both had our driver's licenses.

I'd awoke from a stoned sleep of dreams about a little yellow man with an elephant's head, and lingering memories of when I was a child and my parents and their friends were delving into all kinds of religious' nonsense at which they were hopelessly inept.

I decided to go to the library and do a little investigating on my own. I could have used my mom's card at the university library, but she would have asked all sorts of questions and wanted to help me. I could imagine the pride she'd have about her teachings sinking into my hard head. It was a Saturday afternoon and I rode my bicycle because I didn't want to ask my mom for the car: Where you going why you going who you going with?

The summer rains had been torrential, flooding the Mississippi River and many of its tributaries. Although the sky was overcast, I felt confident I wouldn't be caught in a downpour. Sometimes I had such sensations, as if I could control the weather.

I hadn't been to the library in a long time, and had to ask for help in how to use the computer catalogue. I found out where the section on myths and religions were and decided that browsing would be easier because I wasn't sure what I was looking for in a book. When I got to the area, there was a chick standing in the middle of the aisle, holding one book open, referring to another book open on a shelf, and making notes.

"You're in the way," I said.

"Well, excuse me," she replied, not sounding at all apologetic.

"Why don't you go to a study carol?"

"Why do you have to be so rude?" she asked, looking at me and snatching off her glasses.

"This is a public library: a place for the public."

"We've met before, haven't we? I recognize that surly tone."

It was Esther Miriam. "What're you doing here?" I asked. "What with the bums sleeping all over the place, it's more unsanitary than my swimming-hole."

"What happened to your lisp?"

"Speech therapy. What're you reading?" She showed me the cover. "What, you don't have the *Bible* at home?"

"Oh, let's not start that again. I had dreams about the flood last night and remembered something from class about an older myth than Noah's ark, so I came here to look it up. What about you? I'm surprised you're not out playing baseball kitty."

The previous week some guys from my high school snuck into a homeless shelter for animals and beat several cats to death. I knew who had done it, however, they weren't friends of mine. "I just wanted to look at some pictures."

"In the religious' section?" she asked.

"Yeah. Something about a little creature who writes all the scripts of the world." I shook my head. "I don't really remember. I was just a kid."

"And now you're all grown up."

"Yeah. I'm real mature. I know how to treat people who're blocking my way in the library." She laughed, such a clear tinkling sound, and looked so pretty that I gazed at the floor when I asked, "So how does a guy go about becoming Jewish?"

She touched my forearm, "Are you serious?"

"Maybe. I mean, a minute ago I was thinking the world came into existence by a guy with an elephant's head."

"Our religion isn't that imaginative. Come on, I want to show you something."

She stacked her books on the shelf and led me through the library foyer to the parking lot. She stopped in front of a bright blue car with a sunroof. "Look at my baby," she said. "Isn't it awesome? I probably could have found the right books in my dad's collection, but I wanted an excuse to drive around."

"Yeah. It's all right."

"Philistine," she said. "Hop in and we'll go for a tour."

She put on her glasses and started the engine, backed out, and pulled into traffic. "What're you doing, you spaz? Here, let me. God, I don't need you strangled in my seatbelt the first time I give someone a ride. There you go."

"Hey look! There's Snot!"

"Should we stop?"

"Nah. He's hanging out with a bunch of hoods."

"So how's your summer been?"

"Well, my parents didn't buy me a car but I got drunk for my first time."

"Good for you."

"Yeah. Snot got a homemade tattoo that night. Then his mom called my mom and blamed me."

"Oh? You talked him into it?"

"Nah. I was too busy yakking in the bushes."

"Well," she said, "you're a little old for a bar mitzvah, but they might make an exception."

"What's that?"

"A Jewish party when a young man comes of age. No yakking in the bushes though."

"No tattoos either, I bet." I paused. "So does that mean you'll go out with me?"

She hesitated. "Are you in hurry? I mean, today. Do you have time to go somewhere?"

"Sure." I lied, "I can pick up my car later."

"Oh? You have a car? What kind is it?"

"Just an old beater I bought. But it runs good."

At first it seemed we were out-driving the brewing thunderstorm, but when we reached her house in the suburbs, the rain started pouring down. We ran to the front door and went inside. A woman's voice called from another room, "Esther? Is that you?"

"Yes, mom."

"We don't want you driving in this kind of weather," the voice said, getting nearer. She appeared in the hallway and said, "Oh, you didn't tell me you had company."

"You didn't give me a chance, " Esther said, and introduced us.

"Well, come into the kitchen and have some milk and macaroons. I'll go find your father."

We sat at the kitchen table and I had one of the best cookies I've ever tasted. Esther was uncommonly quiet. Her dad came in and shook my hand, apologizing for being slightly damp. He'd been in the backyard working on the sod for a putting green. He sat down and Esther got him a glass of milk. He asked where I went to school and I told him; then he asked if I had a job.

"I'm a busboy at Durango's."

"Oh, they have fine food there. You could work your way up to being a cook."

"Yeah," I said. "That's part of my plan."

"Do you have plans for college?"

"I'm not sure yet."

"Right, right. It's a torture to get Esther to study for her SATs."

"Oh, dad, I have another year for that."

"That's no reason to put it off, sweetie. More and more students are studying for the SATs and taking them early, which means more competition. Right, Jose?"

"Sure," I said, wondering if the SAT was the same thing my mother had recently been bugging me about. "Yeah," I added, "those tests are really important."

Her dad asked, "Where are you from, Jose? You don't have the air of a native of Madison."

"A small town in Iowa. Stillwater."

"Stillwater, huh? I've never heard of it."

"You're lucky."

He sort of faked a laugh, drank his milk, and told Esther he'd like to see her for a moment in his den. When she returned, I asked, "What was that about?"

"He wanted to know if you're Jewish. And he wasn't too happy about me driving around with a stranger in my new car."

"We're not strangers," I said. "We've known each other for two years."

Esther smiled, "That's what I told him."

"Did you tell him I'll become Jewish?"

She laughed, "If you're serious about that, Jose, call a synagogue."

"You won't help?"

"That's not my forte," she said. "Here, have a stick of gum."

We made out a little while in the library parking lot, then she said she had to go, and to call her if I followed through on converting.

*** *** ***

About the time of high school graduation I got a call from my father in California. He was drunk and feeling guilty.

"Shun," he said, "you should really come out here. No shnow, beautiful women. You could get shtate's reshidency and go to school."

"Is that right, dad? And me living with you would work out all right?"

"Coursh it would, shun. Why? What'sh your mother been telling you?"

"Nothing, dad."

"Well, don't you lishen to her. She'll fill your head with all kinds of crap. She told me you hitchhiked to Minneapolish. What the hell you thinking, shun?"

"I just felt like doing something over spring break."

"Well don't do it again."

"Why not?"

"Faggitsh, shun. They're all over the place."

"Okay. Look. I gotta go, dad. The cat just had puppies and the dog's meowing to be let in."

"Okay, shun. Take care of yourshelf. Itsh not like the old daysh when you could ride around town on yer bishycle and no one bothered you."

"Thanks, dad. I'll keep that in mind."

I went outside and bounced a golf ball off the garage wall for about an hour and then went back inside to look through the stack of SAT applications my mother had brought home. She'd also said she could register me by computer, if I wanted.

I decided to telephone Esther, looked up her last name, and hit the right number on the third try. She took the call in her bedroom where she was packing to go to Israel for a year of school.

"That's kind of dangerous, isn't it?" I asked.

"That's just part of the experience. So you never contacted a rabbi, huh?"

"No, but I have gone kosher."

"Really? Good for you."

"Well, I don't have much choice in the matter. My mom's on a new health food kick, and I'm tired of eating ravioli from a can."

"It's a start. Though I have to say I'm not quite that orthodox."

"What's that?"

"You know…strict."

"Oh. Well, do you think we could see each other before you take off?"

"I don't see how. I've got a million things to do and…well, I'm kind of dating someone."

"Oh," I said; then bitterly, "He's Jewish, right?"

"He sure is," she said brightly, ignoring my tone.

I felt like saying something real mean and derogatory, then I thought about my father and changed tactics. "I guess I was just feeling kind of…you know…lonely."

"Why don't you go out with your friends?"

"Because they're a bunch of flakes. I mean, Snot's still a nice guy but he's got a job lined up cleaning sewers after he graduates. He'll probably spend the rest of his life down there." I didn't mention his new sexual orientation.

"Well, at least he's a nice guy."

"For whatever that's worth."

"Sounds like you're feeling sorry for yourself, Jose."

"I am. Very much so."

"Try reading a good book."

"Like the *Bible*?"

"If that's what works for you. Listen, I gotta go. Call back in another year or two and we'll talk about old times."

We hung up and I dug around under my bed to find the *Bible* I'd kicked there sometime in the previous year.

*** *** ***

After graduation I did a lot of goofing off for about two months. There seemed to be wars everywhere and there was a general concern that a military draft might be invoked. My mom didn't know what to do with me, so she telephoned my dad and he sent a check for a bus ticket to Los Angeles. Snot and I spent it on beer, and when the money ran out, he took his mom's food stamps and began cashing them in for the change.

I dried out for a week at my mom's place, watching cop shows- sponsored by pharmaceutical companies- that told me about the evils of dope. I started hitchhiking west. When I got to Iowa, I caught a ride from an Indian-looking guy on a motorcycle through several states; then we hit Utah, and he turned north, so I had to walk about forty miles through the salt flats. When I got to a suburb of LA, I'm not sure which one, I called my father and he drove out to get me. There was some sort of oil price gouging going on, so he bitched about me being a waste of fuel when he'd sent money for bus fare.

"It's George Bush Junior's revenge, dad."

"What do you mean?"

"He spent twice as much money as Al Gore to win California, something like ten million bucks. And Gore still won the state. You should thank God and the great burning Bush that he hasn't done atom bomb testing at the San Andrea's fault-line and dumped the whole state into the ocean."

"Who told you that? Your mother?"

"I'm only stating the obvious, dad. They guy's more vindictive than Yaweh." He was quiet so I added, "Well, at least he turned the electricity back on. Then blamed it all on a defunct energy company. See, he can be kind and benevolent when he gets the proper adoration."

The next day we had lunch at an outdoor café with his girlfriend and his agent. They talked about some script that my dad was supposedly doing for a studio. His agent said filming was beginning in two weeks, so my father would fly down early to check out the scenery of Peru to make the necessary changes in the script.

We went back to his condo and he said, "Well, son, you want to come along?"

"I've been thinking of enlisting. There might be a draft soon anyway."

"You really want to get involved in one of Bush's crusades?"

"No. But I don't want to go to college either."

"Just come along. We'll expedite your passport tomorrow."

"Okay."

*** *** ***

My dad got drunk on the flight to Lima, Peru and tossed his cookies in the bushes outside the hotel.

"Hey, dad, I'm supposed to be like you, not the other way around." As he crawled further into the shrubbery to escape the audience forming about him, I advised, "Look out for poison ivy!"

I thought that would get it out of his system, but he proceeded to go on a massive binge, which involved going to the worst neighborhoods to buy dope. Due to the War on Drugs, the marijuana and coca plants had been sprayed with some kind of chemical that grew poisonous mold on them. After a week and a half of watching him totter around like a hydrocephalic, I decided I'd had enough. I read his script, sat him down, and gave him martial law.

"Okay, dad," I said, "you're not going out any more. And no booze. I mean, fer chrissake they'll be here in three days to start filming. Hell, you don't even know the difference between Incans and Aztecs."

"It doesn't matter," he mumbled. "They can film either one here."

"How do you know? You haven't even been to their pyramids. Besides, you use both, sometimes in the same sentence. And this Quazicoatl guy who wants to rule the world. I've read something about him and not only is he Aztec, but he's not all evil."

"He is to a Judeo-Christian audience."

"Well, anyway, he's not a pharaoh. How the hell did you get this first draft by the studio?"

"It's a third draft. Or fourth. Oh. I feel terrible."

"Dad, you don't even know what you're smoking. At best it's oregano, but it's probably some fungus. Give me that laptop computer. If they see how awful this is they'll sic the military on us and I don't plan on spending the rest of my life in a concentration camp."

Concentration nee refugee camps had become the world's way of dealing with unwanted populaces. The Jews had them set up around the countries they'd recently kicked ass in, including Lebanon, Syria, and Egypt. As we watched the wars on TV, my father called it a daytime drama, *As The Worm Turns*. The Jews had stretched themselves too thin and the Muslim countries set aside their own differences to attack Israel. A nuclear war seemed imminent.

I didn't have much time to worry about Esther being in Israel because the underclass of Peru were having some sort of revolution. At least that was what I gathered from the military advisors sent down from the United States. I'd gone to a barber and had my hair shaved into a crew-cut so as to fit in with the Yanks. I was a little surprised that both countries would allow filming to go on in a country that was teetering on the brink of chaos.

I'd walked through some of the pyramids and other Incan structures, though at first I had difficulty adjusting to the mountain climate. One of the hotel's maids, a tiny Indian woman, named Inez, who spoke a little more English than I could Spanish- I had two years of it in high school- gave me a massage when she saw how done in I was by the thin atmosphere.

I worked on my father's script and read it to him as he nodded, either in approval or a stupor. It must have been the former because when I finished, he congratulated me.

"Perfect," he said. "But why did you make it Aztec when you bitched about me doing the same thing?"

"Because I did it consistently."

"And having natives be vicariously murdered to run up the body-count was brilliant."

"Expendable casualties," I said.

"That part about making the sexy CIA agent a foul-mouthed, hard-drinking hussy was truly inspired. And saying that her little sister died of some unnamed disease will show that she's not only tough, but sensitive as well."

"Yeah, I thought you'd like that."

"But I'm not sure if the studio will go for the hero dying while saving the world from spaceships."

"We'll just write an alternative ending and let them decide which to film."

"Good idea. Well, son, you've earned your keep. What say we get a bottle of champagne?"

The next day the construction crew arrived and began tearing down foliage around the pyramids they'd chosen to film. They gave out official t-shirts that had the title of the movie to native workers. One of the rivers was too brown so an expert dumped blue dye in it and had the natives collect all the dead fish that floated to the surface. My father referred to the movie people as a swarm of locusts.

I said, "Gee, dad, I didn't know you were so Biblical."

"These are the days that try men's souls."

"I thought you and mom didn't believe in any of that stuff."

"Atheists can suffer apocalypses too, son. Just look around."

"I hate to sound judgmental, dad, but it is how you- and now I- happen to make a living. Why are you oozing sympathy for people you don't even want to know?"

He shook his head. "Just like your mother."

"I thought a little perspective on things might help. We're not here to document the destruction of the rain forest, dad. If you want to console yourself, say that you're an artist."

He looked at me bleakly, "That's something I can't do."

"I don't see why not. Everyone else does. Or are you, as a person once told me, refreshingly honest? Look, if it'll make you feel any better I'll write in a speech for the reporter about the decimation of the environment."

"You don't understand."

"Better than you think I do. I did a paper once for an American history class comparing Moses to Hernando Cortez. I got a D minus."

"Duh. One freed slaves, the other made slaves."

"No, Moses was instrumental in defeating the pagans after the Jews left Egypt. They went in like marauders, killing everyone, except the ones they kept as slaves. Course, it says in the *Bible* the Jews didn't take the pagans' gold or other valuables, but who in their right mind believes that?"

"What's your point, son?"

"They were after new Edens, and they didn't let anyone or anything stand in their way. Call them unenlightened if you want, but everyone has to find a way to support their own versions of paradise."

"Where're you going?"

"I have something to do."

"Can't you stay and talk a while?"

"I've got a date."

That night, as Inez and I lied in my bed, she warned of the revolution, which was to begin soon, and urged me to get on a flight out of Peru. At first I laughed and she became cross, so I promised to leave the next day. I was feeling nauseas anyway and didn't want to watch the movie be filmed.

My father was holed-up with a bottle of bourbon and when I finally got through to him, he said he wanted to stay. He went to the telegram office and had his bank accounts and credit cards placed in both of our names. We said our goodbyes as tanks began rumbling down the streets.

There was no way to get to the airport except to walk. I was in the midst of fleeing people, many of them from the movie, when I was zapped by an overwhelming illness. I stumbled down the back streets, near blind, and followed some railroad tracks out of the city until I was in the jungle.

*** *** ***

I was delirious and in a palsied sweat. I ate bark off trees and overturned rocks for grubs. I lied down to die several times, watching concentric circles spiral from the moon onto me in a small glade where I could see over the tree line. I had visions of an Incan woman laboring in the same spot, where she'd fled from the invading Spanish to give birth.

Eventually, I managed to crawl to a narrow trail where some men on llamas picked me up. They acted as if it were nothing unusual to find a half-dead gringo lying in their path. I'm not sure how many days went by because I spent most of them senseless. We rode out of the mountains and they placed me beside a river.

I was there for a night and woke up the next day to a voice singing in a strange dialect. I crawled closer to the river and saw a woman bathing near the bank. She seemed to keep tune with the birds in the trees above us. I looked down river to see if there was a village, and spotted an elephant playing in the mud. For a moment, it seemed fitting; then I realized I was still sick, as elephants are not indigenous to South America.

Well, at least he hasn't got a human body, I thought. I must have said it aloud, for the woman suddenly turned to me. We stood there for an awkward moment, then she pointed to the mountains and then to me. I nodded and she clapped her hands happily, with an expression of joy on her dark face.

I went down the bank to drink from the river and she gently pulled me into the current. She bathed me and then we lied on the grass and she drained me. "Shiva," she kept saying, as though to encourage me. "Shiva."

Near dusk, she led me back to the trail, pointed to it, and gave me a few soft nudges. When I beckoned for her to join me, she shook her head, traced a circle on her forehead, and pointed to the Andes, where a pillar of light seemed to be shining through the heavens.

I stumbled along for a while, careful to stay on the path. I was ready to give up and crawl or slither like a snake when I heard voices and saw flickers of firelight.

The inhabitants of the fishing village must have been pygmies in prior generations before their genetic stock branched out to other tribes whom had merged with the Spaniards. They were quite short, and friendly enough to feed me for about a week. When they realized I had no assets or talents that could be beneficial to their village, other than putting my own questionable lineage into their genetic pool, they gave me a raft, wrapped some salted fish and roots into leaves, and sent me downriver.

By night I tied the raft to the shore, and by day kept an eye out for rapids and waterfalls. One morning I noticed a charred smell in the air, and rounding a bend saw what must have been a compound of civilization. Wire fences still stood in parts and remnants of the buildings were of cement.

I was still pondering this an hour later when three canoes darted from the bank and began hailing me in what sounded like German. I tried to stop the raft without tipping it over, however, my efforts were in vain. Their voices became more vehement as I drifted away from them. I heard an engine and saw buildings surrounded by wire. A motorboat left the small dock and rushed toward me, nearly overturning the raft in the wake. Two men climbed aboard and grabbed me, screaming in fury.

"Nine sprekan zee Deutch!" I yelled, the only German I had gleaned from a World War II movie that Snot and I had memorized.

That mollified them some, and they tied the raft to the motorboat and steered to the dock, the two goons keeping a tight grip on my emaciated arms.

The next several hours were exceedingly unpleasant. I was led to a small tin shack wherein no light permeated, and was chained to a wall. Not only had I suffered from malaria, but I'd also gotten a dose of dysentery. The mess I was in had the three men who came to get me, a day or so later, dunk me repeatedly in the river.

They took me into a large wooden hall where the smell of the greenness of the logs was sweet enough to have me think I was in a good place. I was made to kneel before a throne, and after about an hour a man appeared from the back recesses of the room and sat before me. He had a patch over one eye and a thick gray beard. He sat on the throne, but wore no crown. He spoke to the attendants and then said, with an accent, "You are American, yes?"

"Yes."

"What is your background?"

"Well, we came to Peru to make a movie, you see, and there was this bloody revolution and I-"

"No no no. We can get into that later. You come from the land of bastards. Your papers are so wadded up that we cannot make out who you are. Tell me, where do your ancestors come from?"

"Ah," I said, realizing it was not the time to take pride in my Irish-Hispanic lineage; excluding them, I said, "Germany."

"How much German?" he asked, leaning forward.

"Oh, I might have a bit of Dutch in me. The family record isn't very clear on that."

He barked orders to the guards who stood me up and unchained my shackles. He turned to me, saying, "Welcome back to your own kind."

"It's good to be here."

*** *** ***

One of the first things they did was get me a tutor in German, for despite being capable in many languages, Wodan was an Anglophobe. It incensed him that England had given up its global empire to side with France in World War II when it was obvious that the Third Reich would have been a better ally; yet if he spoke of Nazi Germany he did so with a hint of sarcastic scorn.

As time went by, and the great hall was filled with tables and chairs, Wodan took to getting me drunk to ply me for information. It usually worked in reverse, for he was a garrulous man, and I wasn't about to tell him I had been born in an Irish Catholic town to one parent who was a New Age spiritualist and another who I was beginning to suspect came from Jewish stock.

Wodan filled me in on things like sub-humans and the Aryan race. The burned out wreck of a compound had been their home until some Zionists had bombed it. "Valhalla going up in flames," he said: "just like Wagner."

Besides keeping some pygmies to do the rebuilding of Wodan's Asgard, he also set them to crafting musical instruments. He issued a decree stating that every German in the compound must learn to play two instruments at a highly adroit level. He also started a printing press so that their stories and myths could be read in future eras. Wodan is many things, but he's no paper-mache Mephistopheles.

One day, between polishing my German and piano lessons, I was helping a guard go for foraging with some pygmies. They were chained together and the first one stepped into quicksand.

"The key," I said, realizing the lead man was probably doomed, but thinking the other three could be saved.

"This is no way to go about selecting a place for an orchard," the guard replied.

"Right. We'd have to drain it. But the key."

"What about it?"

"There's still time to unlock the other three."

"Whoops. You mean two, don't you?"

I held onto the last man as the guard strolled over and flashed the key. I couldn't bear to look into the pygmy's eyes, wide with terror.

I said, "There's a shortage of metal and Wodan will be mad if all the manacles are lost."

The guard nonchalantly freed the slave. The pygmy and I fell onto the grass, gasping for air. The guard smiled at us, picked up the pygmy and threw him in after his fellows.

"He was too close to death to disappoint him."

That night I got drunk and told Wodan the story. He replied, "Never mind. We have a special visitor tonight."

The orchestra struck up some notes from Wagner and a lynx-like man strode in, shimmering into various guises with each step. He stopped before Wodan and the two appraised each other closely; then the visitor waved his hand and the music changed to a sweet harmony.

"Mozart is so much better for the occasion, don't you think?" His voice was sly, yet soothing.

"Ah, our one success from the genetic experiments. Please, Loki, have a seat," Wodan said, indicating an empty chair beside him. "How did your journeys go, my dear foster-brother?"

"Quite well, thank you." He smiled with a hint of contempt. "I see you've succeeded in rebuilding your kingdom."

"Yes, but we lost all the animals."

I drunkenly interrupted, "I think I know where your elephant is."

Loki asked, "And who is this splendid specimen of a walking corpse?"

"A late-comer," Wodan said; "from America."

"Is that right? And your name is?"

"Joseph," I said.

"As in the one bonded into Egypt, or the one who fled there to escape Herod?"

"No. Joseph as in Goebbles."

"My, he is a witty one. But on to business. I have a cargo down river but it will be the last one."

"Oh?" Wodan asked. "And why is that?"

"Ragnorok, dear brother. It's become global. And make no mistake, this will be our last stronghold."

"The Fatherland?"

"In glorious flames," Loki said, relishing the words with a wink to me. "Tell me, brother, did you really go to that Andes' deity and pay him off with an eye just for knowledge? It makes me feel unappreciated."

"Loki, we share many traits, but you are not one known to give advice or wisdom without some sly ends of your own."

Well, Wodan and his crew had a real blast that night. He made all the men turn in their weapons so if a fight broke out they'd only use fists. Early on, I took a cup of mead out to my small quarters, drank it, and went to sleep.

*** *** ***

The next morning I returned to the hall and helped the pygmies clean the place. As I was sweeping the floor, Loki walked in and, kicking slaves out of his way, made directly for me.

"How are you this morning, Joseph? Feeling any better? We sure missed you last night."

"I'm sure you did," I replied, continuing to sweep.

"Ah, doing the runts' job. You know," he said, his voice changing, "they die so easily." I looked at him and for a split-second he had the guise of the guard from the previous day. "Yes," he went on, "they don't seem to take too well to slavery. Not born into it as either slaves to customs of comfort and rituals, nor, I think, deities. What do you think?"

"Loki," I said, holding my head, "what is it you want?"

"Well, I want what you have to offer, except the hangover: you can keep that."

"And what is it you think I can offer?"

"Oh, understanding. Sympathy. Pity. A new life."

"The point, Loki. Get to the point."

"She is here, Jose. She is here."

"Esther? But how?"

"Oh, it took some doing, to be sure. The Syrians were so resolute about having her in one of their brothels. But I used a little finagling with Swiss bank accounts- which probably don't exist any more after what I happened when I ripped off Iran and they went nuclear on the Swiss- then again, Iran doesn't exist either, so it seems to have balanced out."

"Here?"

"As a worker, of course. Head shaved and all that. Our new Asgard needs stronger hands to rebuild it than these dwarves."

"But we couldn't stay here. And you said everything else is destroyed." Loki smiled and I asked, with a glean of hope, "Was that a lie?"

"Not quite. Everything is, indeed, coming to an end. However, we may be able to work a deal with Wodan if you are willing to make a deal with me."

"Well, what do you want?"

"You. As my father."

I sat down at a table and replaced my head in my hands.

"I see you are appropriately stunned."

"No. You remind me of something my mother might say."

"Oh yes. Madison, Wisconsin. They think they're so groundbreaking original there. Ah, but my travels..." He smiled. "You don't even know what you're tempting me with, do you?

I want- I need- new experiences. You know the old adage: He who doesn't learn from history is doomed to repeat it. Well, that's all fine and good unless one is surrounded by dolts who want life to be a perpetual rerun." He shook his head woefully, "If you could only imagine."

"I can Loki. And you've got yourself a deal."

Wodan was more than disappointed when I asked for Esther. "All these fine, buxom Aryan women and you want a Jewess? Here I've taken you in, taught you how to be a proper Nordic figure, and now this?" I let him rage about his throne, keeping quiet while Loki told Wodan that without some new genetic lineages, in several generations Valhalla would be run by sub-morons who couldn't possibly keep the Jews in their subservient place. Loki went on at length about core family values and how Wodan would be the all-father of a brilliant people, summing up:

"I've checked her credentials, my brother, lord, and sire. She's well educated, can play the violin, and this way we'd be sure that he [indicating me] doesn't taint our lineages."

"He's German," Wodan said.

"He says he's German. What proof do we have except his word?"

For obvious reasons I became very nervous and began wondering if Loki was setting me up to be crucified on a double-cross.

"Blonde hair, blue eyes. He's close enough." Wodan let out a sigh. "Well, there's one thing I've learned from history and that is a gene pool should not be a completely closed system."

"Entropy," Loki nodded in agreement.

"Keep her under wraps until her hair grows back and we'll say you saved her from a Jewish prison. That she was sick for a while and had to be doctored. In the meantime, teach her German."

Loki's suspicion that he wouldn't live much longer proved to be correct. He stabbed Wodan's favorite son during a brawl, and was subsequently executed in a painful manner. They rigged some genetic poison and poured it on Loki, and every time he tried to shift shapes to escape, the poison changed too. He went through quite a few forms before he finally expired.

Esther and I are happy- or at least content- with one another. She's become a backstage schemer, attempting to lighten the load for her fellow Jews. At first, Wodan could barely stand to have her in the hall, but recently he seems to take secret delight in her non-stop plotting. I suppose now that Loki's gone, Wodan is sort of lonely for craft and guile.

Some of the scouts reported the fishing village I briefly stayed at, and a military excursion is being planned. Sometimes I think about the dark woman in the river, and wonder what she was after in the Andes. There's been some talk of going into the mountains and using the Jews to mine for gold. When I asked Wodan about Shiva Linga, he traced a circle on his forehead and kept quiet.

A few days ago I took our son away from Esther as she recited some passages she'd memorized about *Genesis* and Jacob. She got mad and stormed off. I sat my boy on my knee and told him, "In B.C.C., Before Computers and Cable, there was a ritual known as cartoon watching. Every Sabbath, that is Saturday morning, children would wake up early and turn to their shrine to get lessons of tricks from rascals who were in the forms of animals. The greatest one was a rabbit..."